Bang Baby
Sophie MacDonald
Copyright Sophie MacDonald 2013
Published at Smashwords

This Is a Work of Fiction *involving an incest theme with consenting adults, and produced for adult entertainment only. If you do not agree with an adult incest theme do not read this story.*

All characters are over 18. All names, characters, places and incidents are used fictitiously. Any resemblance to actual events or locales or persons, living or dead, is entirely coincidental.

You MUST be over 18 years old to read this story. If you are under 18 or do not wish to view adult content, you must exit now. _Adults Only._

Share your thoughts with us.
Take a moment to tell us how we're doing. Your feedback really matters.

You can reach us by:
Email: **_my777books@yahoo.com_**

Search for other titles by **Sophie MacDonald.**

Bang Baby

Chapter 1
Open Pandora's Box or A little peek inside couldn't hurt.

Tony and Rachel Anderson had been married for nineteen years. They had gotten married when Tony was twenty-one and Rachel was nineteen. They had met and began dating when Tony was in his last year of high school and kept on dating while he was in college. They met the summer Rachel turned sixteen. It was a whirl wind summer romance full of lust, laughter and love. They kept dating in spite of the age difference, their peers' thoughts and their parent's initial objections. They were actually very much in love and completely devoted to one another. Tony had always intended on marrying Rachel and the fact that she had gotten pregnant with their son Michael just moved his agenda along a little quicker. With the exception of twelve years ago when Tony had a little 'Mid-Life Crisis' their relationship was pretty solid and on a good footing. Like all married couples who have been together that long their sex life had become somewhat predictable and practiced. That's when Rachel chose to take a decidedly new tact to kick things up a notch and make their sex life just a little more spicy.

Sex was still good and they both enjoyed it immensely however, the lusty spark was gone. Rachel still found her husband attractive. He was tall, six foot, still had all his hair, although he wore it shorter and it was more of a salt pepper grey than the dark brown of his youth. He was only slightly overweight but reasonably fit and marginally active. He didn't do Yoga on a daily basis like she did but he walked and rode his bike faithfully. He had the most beautiful blue eyes she had ever seen on anyone. Her son Michael also had the same colour blue to his eyes and they were just as deeply set and piercing as his dads. In fact except for the hair, Michael's being jet black, he was the spitting image of his father only slightly taller and maybe a bit stockier than his dad was at his age. He probably got that from her side of the family as Rachel's father was a big man standing well over six feet four. Rachel herself was a stunning woman. She stood five feet four inches tall had a sexy curvaceous figure much like her mother, with firm full breasts, hips and an ass. When they were younger her husband had told her, that her ass looked like she was built for fucking. Of course he hadn't spoken to her like that in years and that was one of the things she was hoping to change in the near future.

Her legs were fantastic. They were long and shapely, giving her the illusion of being taller than she actually was, with gorgeous calves and thighs that beautifully moulded themselves into that succulent ass of hers. Her ass was one of her best features and she often bragged to her husband that you could bounce a quarter off of it, especially when she caught him looking at it and thought she wasn't paying attention. She often wore a bra although she didn't need to and in fact usually on weekends went without one. On weekends she traded her high heels, sharp business skirts, blouses and suit jackets for jeans and T-shirts. If she could go barefoot most of the time, she would, choosing to wear open toed sandals that showed off her beautiful feet and ankles. Again when they were younger her husband had a bit of a foot fetish and often had her wear high heeled shoes that were open toed strap affairs that help accentuate her feet, ankles and sexy calves. He used to buy her high heeled sandals with straps that went up her legs around her calves, tying off just below the knee. This too had died somewhere in their past and she missed the attention he had lavished upon her. The shoes were not often the quality she normally wore but it was the thought that mattered most to her.

She loved her family. Loved her husband and loved sex but she wanted more. So as with most things, if change was going to come she would have to be the one to initiate it. She decided she would be brave and put herself and her desire out there for her husband to respond to, she didn't know what would come of it, but something was better than nothing. They were in a rut and things needed to change.

"Tell me one of your kinkiest fantasies" she said plainly.

They hadn't been having sex for very long when she asked the question. Her husband's hard cock was buried inside her, her legs were spread wide and wrapped around his hips allowing him complete access to her, she loved being open to him. He had both hands on her breasts and had been gently licking and kissing her neck, every once in awhile pausing to lick and suck her left nipple, nothing out of the ordinary. This was their routine; in fact this was their sex night. Sunday night, weekend was over, it was after 9 p.m. and nothing much was left to watch on T.V. This was how it was and this was how their sex life went, week in and week out. So what better time to ask a question that she felt needed to be asked? They needed change, they needed something. Spice, excitement, the edge just like when they were young, this is what she wanted from him and she was bound and determined to get it, come hell or high water.

"Here? Right now?" Her husband responded stopping in mid thrust to look his wife in the eyes, something he rarely did when they made love.

"Yes, here and right now." She replied, a slight annoyance in her voice. "I wouldn't have asked if I didn't want to know or think it was important."

She brushed a stray hair from her face that was tickling her nose and causing her to blink repeatedly. She needed to be taken seriously, this was important.

"But we're making love." That was probably the dumbest thing he could've said at that moment and hindsight being what it is, he knew it, not ten seconds after he said it.

"I know we're making love." Rachel said curtly. She was beginning to get more annoyed and it was now starting to show in how she held her body.

"Ok, ok. Well I like it when you shave." Tony said blushing moderately with his eyes cast down. "Or have a little landing strip. That might be nice."

The pause and silence that followed felt ominous and he knew this wasn't fully what she was asking. But he was on the spot and somewhat embarrassed with the flood of thoughts that began to race through his mind once he began to consider what she had asked.

"Well that can be fun but it's not kinky, and it's not really a fantasy is it?" Rachel said and began pressing for more. "What really gets you going? Turns you on, you know edgy stuff, out of the ordinary, kinky."

"Oh kinky, well I'm not sure." Tony was on shaky ground now. He wasn't really sure what she wanted and he really wasn't sure how far to go. He had kinky thoughts of course everyone did but usually they were fleeting and as quickly as they came into his head he dismissed them.

"Don't tell me you don't surf the net when you're bored. You can't be that much of a workaholic." She pried further, she knew he looked at porn, read erotica; they both did from time to time. "When you're in the den and on the computer, what's the kinkiest thing you've ever looked at or fantasized about?"

Rachel was pushing a little bit harder than was normal for her but she wanted them to get past this humdrum rut they were in and move onto something more exciting, sexy and hot.

Now he was embarrassed. Tony wasn't sure where to go with his thoughts, he was confused and nervous. 'What if I say something that's weird or abnormal and she thinks

I'm just plain perverted.' He thought. He slid his cock out of his wife and lay on his back looking blankly at the ceiling.

"Look Hun, I didn't mean to start an argument". She said, rolling on her side facing him. "All I wanted to do was add a little spice to our sex life."

Her hand was tracing small circles on his chest. Little figure eights that she gently ran up and down his chest, periodically touching his nipples then moving sensually down to his stomach. She was attempting to reassure him through touch that everything was alright, men have such frail egos and she didn't want the moment to be lost.

"Are you saying I bore you?"

"No that's not what I'm saying at all. For Christ-sake Tone what day is it?" she sounded exasperated now and Tony really didn't know what to do or say.

"Sunday, why?" he replied, now completely confused.

"Of course it's Sunday! We always have sex on Sunday. Sometime after nine when nothing is on T.V. that you want watch, you turn off the damn set, lean over like clockwork and nibble on my neck. My right ear to be precise. You crawl on top of me, I spread my legs. Off comes the pyjamas, off go my underwear, down goes your hand, three or four strokes of my clit and pussy to get me wet and in slides your cock." It was a bit of a rant but it was true, she didn't pull any punches.

"Oh I see." He replied softly, not sure whether to run and hide or begin apologizing profusely.

"Oh I see, is that it. Nineteen years of marriage and all I get is, Oh I see!" Now she was sounding fully annoyed.

"Well I didn't know I bored you." He continued, "I thought you loved me and I loved you."

Ok now he was defensive and this was precisely what she didn't want. This was far from what she envisioned. He'd share some of the wall fantasy, she'd share one of hers, they'd role play a bit and they'd move into a new and more exciting direction.

"You don't bore me." She was starting to get exacerbated. "I'm simply trying to spice up our marriage. Do remember how it was when we were first married. Better yet, when we were dating, do you remember? You fucked me in my parent's basement, in the laundry room the first time my parents had you over for dinner. Hell you fucked me twice as I recall. I had to sit through dinner with your cum soaking my panties. There was no way anyone sitting close to me couldn't smell our sex." The emotion of all her pent up frustration was beginning to show.

"You sat at the end of the table by your mom." Tony responded.

"Precisely, who do you think sat me there?" She stared at him and continued. "Normally I sat by my father. Oh that would've gone over well. Me, with a cunt full of cum and you with no testicles, Happy Thanksgiving kids! He'd have killed you. My mom was saving my life and yours."

"Honey you said the 'C' word." He was genuinely shocked. Sure she swore before but not often. And to use the 'C' word, that just didn't come out of his wife's mouth easily.

"Well I'm frustrated what do you want." She said plainly. "There are a whole bunch of words I should be saying. I like dirty talk you should try it."

He stared at her unable to believe what he was hearing. Who is this person and what have they done with my wife.

"Really like what?" he questioned not sure he wanted to hear the answer.

"Like slut, whore, bitch, cock, cunt, pussy for starters." She through a litany at him, all the words she wanted to hear. All the words she wanted to say. All the words you would never say unless you were having wild passionate sex. Words you would scream at the top of your lungs as your partner rocked your world and took your breath away. Words that would make you have to apologize to your neighbours the next day or at the very least blush when you saw them, because you knew they'd heard you.

"Don't you find some of those words degrading?" he said, looking at her calmly.

"Sure I do but not when we're having sex. Then it's different." She looked him straight in the eyes, ensuring he was hearing her and that they were definitely connecting. She didn't think she would have the courage to have this conversation twice, at least not be the one to initiate it again. "Then we're fucking. There I said it."

There was a bit of pause before she began again. "Fucking! Fucking. Fucking. Fuck, fuck, fucking." She immediately flopped back onto the bed, her head smacking into the pillow causing it to fluff out exaggeratedly. "God why can't you just fuck me? Throw me to the bed and fuck the shit out of me! Don't worry about if I cum or not. Just throw me down spread my legs and fuck me, who cares if I'm wet. I'm your bitch and I'll get wet."

She turned and stared straight at him. Her eyes wide, her nostrils flaring as she continued her rant. "After ten or twenty thrust you'll make me wet. You'll cum deep and hard inside, from behind. You'll pull my hair. You'll slap my ass, and when you're done, you'll flip me over stick your wet dick in my mouth and say good night."

"Oh my." Was all he could say. He didn't know what to do. Part of him was in shock, not sure how to respond. He was overwhelmed. He had no idea she felt these things, thought these things or wanted these things. Yes part of him didn't know what to do and another part of him wanted to do exactly what she said.

"Ok I've told you my thoughts what are yours chief, and don't give me that shaved pussy bit cause as of tomorrow it'll be bald."

They sat in silence for maybe five minutes, although it felt ten or twenty times longer to Tony. He stared at the ceiling his mind reeling from what he had just heard. It was a lot to take in and it wasn't easy to process. He was aroused that was for sure, his erection didn't seem to want to go away. But still he was not in his comfort zone. Rachel on the other hand appeared unusually calm and somewhat content. She had just purged herself of all the frustration she had pent up inside her and was breathing in the calm that comes from riding yourself of a weight that was threatening to burry you.

"Well Tone." She said as she began to move to his chest, placing gentle kisses around his nipples. She added the odd nibble and bite as she moved over his body straddling him. His cock rested between her legs, he could feel the heat coming off her sex. Slowly she began to slide her pussy up and down the length of his cock. She was leaving a wet glistening trail along his shaft. She held herself in balance over just allowing enough pressure for her labia to gently caress his.

"What turns you on, gets you going? Huh Tone." Her voice was soft and seductive, with an airy hush to it. Her hips were moving up and down his length, with just barely the suggestion of a fuck. She wasn't giving him enough to get off just enough to tease and provoke.

"What makes that cock hard Tone? I know you're thinking something I can see it in your eyes." He was thinking something. Something dark and erotic but not quite formed. It involved her and her sex. Her and her pussy. Her and her cunt. God now she was getting him to use the 'C' word if only in his thoughts. His eyes closed, he imagined her firm full breasts with their hard nipples showing her excitement. Her body writhing in ecstasy as waves of pleasure coursed through her.

"You're horny lover." She placed soft gentle kisses on his lips, and settled back down across his hips. His cock and balls glistened with her juice. Her clit was hard and protruding from her body. It began to expose itself, coming out from under its protective hood. He was rock hard; she reached down between her legs and began to touch his cock. Not to stroke it but merely to touch it and trace her fingernails along the shaft up to the tip and just under the ridge of the purple swollen head. She paused there tracing the shape the head with her finger, moving it to the tip where a copious amount of precum was leaking from his urethra. He was hard alright. Hard and his balls were tight and aching, she hadn't seen him like this in a while and she liked it. She leaned forward again, pressing her hard little clit into his shaft grinding it harder into him. This was for her pleasure now. She leaned closer to him again, placing a small kiss on his mouth, licking his lips with her tongue.

Again she began to speak. She was going to take him to the edge. Show him how to get there but not push him over, he could do that himself. "Yeah your balls are tight and your cock is hard. You got a nasty thought in there baby? You got a nasty thought for mommy."

"Tell mommy what you like. You feel how wet she is, how hot she is. Tell her what you want to do her." She continued pushing the edge. His chest was beginning to heave up and down as his breathing quickened. His body was vibrating; he was on the edge alright. As soon as she began to use the word mommy something within him reacted on an almost visceral level.

"That's it baby, tell me. Tell me what you're thinking and you can fuck me with that nasty cock. Tell me that deep dark thought. Let me hear it baby I'm a whore, a slut you won't shock me. Feel how wet my cunt is baby? It's for you baby, this nasty whores cunt is all for you." Again she pressed into him grind her clit against his stiff cock. She was soaking him. She didn't know how much longer she could keep this up her own orgasm was eminent, threatening to cascade through her body.

"Oh fuck little boy, tell this bitch what you want. Share your thoughts and you can fuck her. Tell her damn it! Tell her. You have a nasty thought for me don't you baby? Don't you?"

"Yes!!" he growled as he grabbed her in a sudden movement that took both of them off guard. In one quick turn he scooped her up in his arms, pulled her tightly into his body and flipped her on her back. Her legs went flying up in the air and he flung them over his shoulders. He slid his cock between the lips of her sex, separating her labia causing the head of his cock to rub against her exposed clit. She moaned wildly as he did so. He stroked himself back and forth across the lips of her pussy, smearing her juice all over the underside of his rigid cock.

"That's it lover tell me what you're thinking. What nasty, dirty thoughts are going through the beautiful mind of yours? What's daddy got in mind for mommy?"

He continued to stroke his cock through her lips, gently pushing down more and more. Not enough to penetrate her but enough to cause her ripples of pleasure and begin to stimulate her hardening clit further. She was so close now; she knew she didn't have long.

"Tell me babe." She continued, "Tell me what nasty dirty thing you want to do. How can this slutty bitch serve you?"

"I want to see you fucked." He roared as he drove his cock deep into her cunt. There was no preliminary waiting for her to adjust to his presence. He just thrust his cock into her as deep as he could go and ground their pubic bones together. Her little clit was mashed tightly to him and set ripples of pleasure through her body. Her legs wrapped tightly around him as she ground back against him. This was fucking. "I want to see you fucked by a big hard cock that stretches that tight pussy of yours."

He pulled back and then slammed forward. Almost all the way out and then back in. He did this twice more to accentuate the feeling of his cock slamming into her. His thrusts were becoming more and more exaggerated. The walls of her vagina were wet and slick and accommodating each hard thrust. Her hips were moving to meet with his. She was grinding her pussy into him while at the same time swirling her hips so that her vaginal walls could squeeze the shaft of his rigid cock.

"I want you fucked hard and filled full of cum." He growled as he pushed her legs back to her chest causing breasts to push forward. Her knees were up near her shoulders pressed tight against her body. He could hear the air escaping from her lungs as drove his hard shaft into her. Her body was reeling from the fucking she was receiving. Her eyes rolled back into her head as she felt the wave begin. A continual stream of incoherent moaning was escaping from her. Her mouth began to gap open, her head tilted back exposing her neck in a sexy arch that began from there and moved down her body as she arched her back in ecstasy.

"I want to have you fucked by someone else with a big cock and then I want to fuck you when there done." He couldn't believe what he was saying to her. This was his wife and he wanted her to be slutty, to be a whore to be just a cunt. Fuck well and abused and filled with cum and then he wanted to fuck her.

After the first wave passed Rachel came back to reality and regained her ability to speak. She knew she needed to reinforce what they were doing give her approval let him know this was ok. This was what she wanted from him. "Oh god baby, that's it fuck me! Fuck this bitch with the nasty wet pussy." Rachel was ecstatic. Finally Tony was fucking her. Not in an inexperienced teenage lover kind of way which was hot but in an adult male I know a little more about what I'm doing kind of way.

"That's it baby tell me more. Tell me more."

"I want sloppy fucking seconds." He was thrusting into her rapidly now. Both of his hands were holding her ankles as he continued to thrust in and out of her. He was stretching her wide apart and was rutting into her like some wild animal. When he wasn't talking he was grunting. Her cunt, for that what it was now, was engorged with arousal, it was wet and sloppy. His cock and balls were slick with her love juice. As he looked down at this gorgeous hot woman below him he was so in the moment that he began to believe the fantasy. She was a slut, a whore he was fucking who had already been fucked and after he was done she was going to go out and fuck again. She was a wild feral feline women exuding raw sexual energy and he was there to serve her and move on once he was done, once she was done.

Rachel couldn't believe the reaction she was getting from Tony. This was fucking. His hard cock was sliding in and out of her. It felt good and strong and rigid. She wanted to break it off and leave it inside her like this. The hard maleness of it made her feel sexual and feminine. Not in a soft demure kind of way but in an erotic wild way. Her pussy was wet and sloppy; its lips were plump and full. God her clit was hard she was almost afraid to touch fearing she would explode. Waves of pleasure moved through her body and radiated out. Her nipples were diamond hard points and she took them in each of her hands and twisted and pulled them. God she love the slight feeling of slight pain combined with pleasure that she got when she twisted them in her fingers.

"Oh my Tony you're going to make me cum." It came up on her suddenly. She knew it was there, her orgasm, but had thought it was still a little ways off. A heat began in the centre of her stomach and moved outward, then waves started almost like and itch you can't scratch, not quite a burning sensation but the warmth began to flood her body. Burning needles of fire and she was cumming, her orgasm hit and she began to cum.

"Oh fuck Tony don't stop baby keep fucking me. That's it honey make me cum baby make me cum. I'll be a bitch baby. I'll be a slut; you can have a whore cunt full of cum. Just don't stop fucking me, keep fucking me. That's it you prick make me cum and then add you cum to his."

That was all it took Tony couldn't take any more. Rachel vaginal walls began to spasm and grip his cock. Her body began to shake, her eyes rolled into the back of her head and she exploded right before him. His stiff hard prick began couldn't take any more. The head of his cock was too sensitive and there was no stopping what was happening he was going to cum and cum hard. He began to spew rope after rope of cum into his lovely wife who in a matter of minutes went from bitch, slut, and whore back to his wife and he was lost in the beauty and raw sex appeal that was her.

They lay there exhausted. He was still on top of her breathing heavy, she below him, legs spread, arms above her head, her chest rising and falling as her body attempted to re-oxygenate itself. His cock slowly going flaccid and falling from her sex. There fluids pouring from her like when a cork leaves a bottle resting on its side. The room smelled of sex, god she loved that smell. It was the thing that turned her on the most. There was no escaping what happened in this room the smell gave it away. Even in the post coitus afterglow of an amazingly strong orgasm the smell mad her horny and clouded her judgement.

"Baby if I could find you a big cock would you take it?" He was nervous now. She had opened a door he had been afraid to open because he knew where it might lead, where he wanted it to go and it was nasty.

"If it meant you'd fuck the hell out of me just like you did tonight I might consider it." Her mind was still clouded and she wasn't done feeling horny. Her pussy throbbed at the loss of his cock. Oh she may be sore in the morning but right now in this moment she wasn't and if he could go again she'd consider it.

"Seriously?"

"Easy there tiger. Honey I love you. You are it for me and right now I'm very satisfied. If you want to go again and thinking of me taking on a big cock and having it shoved deep up my cunt will get you there then I'm your girl. But lover I just found you again and I'm keeping you." She tried to emphasize the 'you.' She didn't know where he was going and recognized she was too vulnerable to play. They were experimenting and she needed to keep things safe. The one thing she knew about her husband was that he was an all or nothing type of guy. And that sometimes lead him to jump into the deep water with his eyes closed.

Chapter 2
Taking the tiger by the tail, or hold on for the ride.

They fell asleep beside each other each somewhat spent and exhausted but content. At three-thirty in the morning Rachel was startled awake as her legs and hips were pulled to the middle of the bed.

"Oh you fucking bitch you're at it again." Her husband was looming above her on the bed. His cock was hard and erect, ready for action. He was on his knees before and had spread her legs wide apart and was looking at her sex. It was gaping slightly from the fucking she had received earlier in the evening. Her pussy still wet and glistening with the mix of juices, hers and his. She knew he was role playing that they weren't his and he was chastising her for her sluttish behaviour.

"Look at you, your cunt it's full of cum." His voice sounded somewhere between a mix of cross and heighten arousal. "You've leaked it all over the bed you whore."

"Well the way I see it baby you have a few options. You can either lick it out of me so I don't end up pregnant again. You can fuck me and add your own to an already sexy mess. Or you can punish me and try and convince yourself that when you're done I won't do it again, but you know damn well I will." She smiled as she spoke. It had been years since they had, had sex twice in one night and if this little dramatic role play was going to ensure that she was damn well going to fulfill her role as the wanton hussy.

"Well as I see it how about we do all three?" He said as drove his hard cock deep into the center of her heated pussy.

"Oh my, it looks like it's my lucky night." Her smile broadened and her eyes lit up with glee. He stroked himself inside her for six hard thrusts and then pulled out. His cock glistening with the remnants of her lust. He paused only slightly as if considering his choices and then dove face first into her center.

"Oh god you are a horny devil." She wailed as dove face first into her sex, his face splitting her open and his tongue penetrating the folds of her sex. He roared and groaned loudly as his body shuddered. He ate her with a vengeance, sucking and licking her center. At first he stuck his tongue in her as deep as he could get licking and suck the remnants of their love. The he move up and found her clit poking out of its hood hard and proud. He began swirling his tongue in a clockwise motion around and over the hard nub of flesh. Rachel's nerve endings went wild. Her hips thrust up into his face without so much as a thought or consideration from her; she was completely instinctual in that moment. She attempted grind his face into her body rubbing herself up and down his face from his chin to his forehead. He was covered with her juice and he loved it. Rachel's body began to spasm and shake, her orgasm beginning to take hold. At that point Tony pulled his face out of her and replaced his tongue with his cock. He was a wild man. He grabbed and squeezed her breasts, twisting her nipples and then bringing his mouth down on each nipple which voraciously sucked and then bit. Soon his mouth came to hers. He grabbed her chin with his right hand placing two fingers in her mouth to hold her jaw open as he kissed and suck her tongue. They shared a powerful kiss and the taste and smell of pussy and semen permeated their senses.

The sex was passionate but quick and it ended with Tony fucking her from behind as he slapped her ass. As Rachel's first orgasm ended Tony pulled out of her and rolled her over onto her stomach, spread her legs and drove his cock into her from behind. Rachel's arms flew forward and she braced herself against the head board. Her head and shoulders were flat against the bed, her hips and ass were thrust upward to meet her husband and allow him complete access to her ever accepting vagina. She screamed in joy and rapture as she felt him release inside her as four pronounce spurts from his cock bathed her cervix with his seed.

As he came in her he was raging things like "Where'd you fuck him bitch, in our bed or his" followed by, "It was him wasn't it. You've become such a whore for his big cock haven't you bitch, haven't you?" And then, "What if you are pregnant? You made me get fixed and now you're full of his cum." She was so caught up in her orgasm that she didn't play along as well as she could have, so she really didn't know where he was going with all his implied references. That and the fact that Monday was a work day and she would be so damn tired as it was she just didn't have the energy to keep the role play going.

That morning was wonderful. Yes they were tired but every time one of them looked at the other they were both blushing like teenagers.

They each went independently about their routines. Tony went to the kitchen to make toast and coffee. Rachel jumped in the shower to clean up and get ready for her day. By the time he came back to the bedroom Tony found Rachel out of the shower and dressed except for her jacket, she had on her dark black pencil skirt with the pin stripe and a white bloused. She was stepping into a pair black three inch heels that set off her nylon covered legs perfectly. She was putting in her earrings adjusting her hair and makeup. She was fascinatingly beautiful.

"Coffees made and everything is out for toast. Whole wheat?" He said as he headed straight into the shower.

"Thanks babe you're perfect."

When he came into the kitchen again, this time dressed in his suit and tie, he found her leaning against the counter drinking her coffee. She had put away the toaster, jam and peanut butter and cleaned off the counter. She looked at him over the cup of coffee her eyes filled with a mischievous glint.

"Did you shave this morning?" She asked. He nodded, at the rather benign question until she added, "Me too."

Immediately his face flushed as he recalled what she had said last night 'cause as of tomorrow it'll bald.' He quickly moved in to her, pressing her against the counter. His need to find out for himself over powered his common sense. His heart raced as he pushed his hand past the top of skirt and slipped it under the waist band of panties to feel her almost bald pussy. "I decided on a landing strip, unless you disapprove?"

His face flushed a deeper red now, making his excitement easily readable to anyone in the room. He cupped her sex with his whole hand, his fingers finding and making out every detail, her vulva, with its outer and inner labia, which were starting to moisten. The opening of her vagina, it was soft and wet, he could feel the heat coming of her sex. The protective hood of her clitoris and finally her little clit, which was just beginning to harden. Just then she suddenly twisted her hips and moved to the side dislodging his hand from her skirt. She grabbed his wrist and brought his fingers to her mouth. They both could smell her sent. Gently she sucked his fingers clean and then walked away smiling. "I thought a landing strip was more appropriate. After all a busy runway that might get a big over sized jet visiting it and you certainly would want something there to guide it in and let it know where it belongs."

Before he could respond their son Michael entered the kitchen in his T-shirt and boxers. Tony kept facing the counter for fear he would reveal the erection he currently had in his pants. Clearly it was too early in the morning for Michael as he staggered to the fridge opened the door and got the milk, then turned headed for the kitchen table only to turn around again and grab the cereal off the top of the fridge. Placing both items on the table he turned around and looked at his parents who were blocking his way to the bowls and spoons.

"I thought you two would've had enough of each other last night."

His dad was the first to respond "Hey..."

But Rachel cut him off. "Did we keep you up? Sorry about that baby your father couldn't keep his hands off of me." She smiled at her husband over her cup of coffee. Her eyes bright and perfect, she was never lovelier, more vibrant.

"Ah gross mom. Can I have a bowl and a spoon?"

She knew the easiest way to avoid an embarrassing situation was to meet it head on. Take the embarrassment right out of it by eliminating any power it might hold over you. She reached back and opened the silverware drawer grabbed a spoon and reached up into the cupboards and got out a cereal bowl. "There you go a regular Jethro Boudine bowl for my starving boy."

"Ha ha, funny funny mom. Don't you have work?"

"Yes dear we all can't have the summer off to frolic and swim. Sitting round in our underwear stinking up the whole house."

"I have Training Camp today and coach doesn't let us rest." Michael had been accepted to university on a baseball scholarship, but needed to maintain his skill set. The university had recommended a summer program so between that and his part time job so he really was quite busy. Rachel knew this was a bone of contention for him and just liked to give him a hard time about plying all summer rather than working.

She gracefully moved by both her men and picked up some file folders that were lying on the counter by the fridge. "Time to make the doughnuts." She laughed at her own humour as she headed out the door.

Tony regained his composure and left for work as well. He would be horny all day.

Throughout the day both Rachel and Tony found their thoughts drifting to the previous night's activity. Tony's own thoughts went from extreme arousal to embarrassment and back, while Rachel's went from arousal to worry she'd pushed too far, with only touches of embarrassment, mostly hoping Tony wouldn't remember everything she had said but knowing full well he would.

Rachel was the first to get home, or so she thought. As she came in the house she headed immediately for her bedroom and the couples en-suite bath and shower. She had shaved that morning and found herself with an uncomfortable itch. She was headed to her bedroom to find some lotion of some kind to relieve the burning and she didn't want an unsightly rash. Driven by the desire for relief she began to disrobe along the way. She had left her blazer in the kitchen on hanging on a chair and had pulled her blouse loose from the waist of her skirt, she undid all the buttons of the blouse leaving it hanging open and headed up the stairs as she kicked of her shoes and flung them down the hall. She had just unzipped the back of her skirt as she continued down the hall, letting it fall to the floor, and turned into her room. She began to pull her panties down when she heard the noise. "Oh fuck!"

Michael had come home early after practice and had decided to use his parents shower, it had four shower heads with multiple massage settings, so he really enjoyed using it after practice. The shower was shutting off and Michael was coming out of the bathroom when his mother was going in.

"Whoa! Mom! Sorry, oh my god, sorry." He tried to turn back around and avert his eyes. As he twisted and jumped back he ran head long into the door frame. "Fuck!"

Michael's head careened off the door frame with an awful thunk! He immediately dropped his towel and grabbed his forehead. Realizing this now left him exposed, he panicked again; he was naked in front of his mother, he reflexively reached down for his towel and smacked his elbow on the bathroom counter, then slipped and landed on his butt with and awful thud.

"Ok, ok stop!" His mother commanded. Michael looked up at his mom realizing she was pretty much naked. "Alright, before you kill yourself, grab your towel and put it around your waist. I'm going to get my house coat and we're both going to cover up."

'She shaved her snatch' Michael thought 'My mother shaves her snatch. Oh my god. Oh my god.' He was blushing as he pulled his towel around his waist, he needed to relax and get his bearings. Just relax and keep your eyes down, just breathe 'why'd you have to stare right at her crotch' he admonished himself. He had a myriad of thoughts going through his brain and none of them were good.

"Michael. Michael! Look at me I need to look at your head." He was looking at the ground as she spoke. She needed to get his attention and assess his injuries. "Look at me young man."

As he looked up he saw that she was now wearing her housecoat. She was somewhat more presentable, although her ample cleavage was more than apparent. The fact that he knew she was naked from the waist down didn't help. 'Oh god she doesn't even have her nylons on, and her toes are painted. Oh fuck she has the sexiest feet and ankles. When did she start wearing an anklet?' His mind was racing.

"Ok we need to get an icepack on that head of yours, come with me." He dutifully followed his mother. Even at the age of nineteen some things are just ingrained and conditioned. Your mother tells you to move, you move -- Resistance is Futile. It was always a running joke with her, she would use a mock voice anytime he even so much as tried to invoke any pretence of his own authority 'I am your mother. Resistance is futile.'

Once in the kitchen she sat him down, got a wash cloth from the drawer beside the sink, wet it and wiped his forehead cleaning his brow. "Ok, the skin isn't broken but you're going to have a nasty bruise and some swelling. Hold this. Michael are you listening to me."

She left the facecloth on his forehead and he robotically did as instructed. She turned and went to the kitchen cupboard and began looking for something. Not finding it right away, she bent over and began looking through the bottom cupboards.

"There you are." She exhaled, and pulled out a box of plastic freezer bags that were sealable. She selected one and then turned and went to the freezer to retrieve some ice cubes. Placing the ice cubes in the plastic bag and sealing it up she returned to him and reached out for the cloth and said, "Gimme."

Throughout this whole ordeal Michael was having a hard time not looking at his mother in a completely different way. Oh sure he had known she was pretty, none of his friends had let him forget it. When he was younger, in grade nine, he had gotten into a fight with his best friend at the time, Ronnie Allen. Ronnie had made an offhand comment about wanting to bone her, in front of Matthew Peterson, Paul Arnold and Robbie McMasters. Michael had gotten so angry he ploughed him right in the nose breaking it. They haven't spoken since. He was starting to think that maybe he had been a little too hard on him. God he couldn't focus every move she made had a sexual feel and overtone to it, he had to get himself under control before it became embarrassing.

Rachel felt flushed. What was wrong with her, she kept staring at Michael's crotch. It didn't help matters that her pussy had been itchy all day from shaving it and she'd therefore walked around with a constant reminder of last night's activities. She was buzzing all day from the sexual play she and her husband had gone through and was dying for more. But seeing Michael's crotch and what hung between his legs had thrown her just a bit. It wasn't like he had an erection and maybe that was part of the problem, he wasn't erect but he was still big. Soft he was as big if not a little bigger than Tony. "Ok I think you'll be alright. Go to your room and get dressed and supper will be ready by six, were having Hamburgers. Dad's Barbecuing."

There she thought nice redirect. 'Focus on a task and mention his father and we can move forward. Everything is back to normal.'

Tony was home not twenty minutes later. As soon as he walked in the door Rachel grabbed him by the hand and dragged him into their bedroom. Shutting the door she immediately went for his belt and began to undo his pants. Getting frustrated with the buckle she swore. "Fuck. Get that thing undone now, I need you."

"Oh my whats gotten into you?" Tony wasn't resistive really, just taken aback by her very forthright presentation.

"Nothing, I tell you later... if you're lucky." She was on her knees looking up at him and then she stared straight ahead. His buckle was now undone so she undid the button to his pants, pulled the zipper down, letting his pants fall to the ground. She pulled his underwear down to his knees, grabbed hold of his cock and held it briefly in her hand. "There you are, come to momma."

Immediately she opened her mouth and took him completely. Soon he began to grow and harden, his length no longer fitting her mouth and pushing toward her throat. She released him with a gasp of air and licked and kissed the head and shaft, reassessing his size. Opening her mouth she took him again sucking and swallowing as she did. This time when his cock reached the back of her throat she held herself steady. Placing both hands on his hips she held him in place and pushed forward. He could feel the head of his cock hitting the back of her throat, where it seemed to stop. Amazingly Rachel continued forward and he could feel the head of his cock entering her throat. The sensation was incredible, she had given him head before of course but she had never taken him so deeply. Still she moved forward and stopped. He could hear her gag and begin to choke. She immediately backed off and brought her mouth off his shaft. With a gasp of air she spoke. "FUCK! Almost just a bit further and you'll be past my gag reflex. I'm going to make you cum so hard."

She began to lick his shaft again, breathing in his musky sent. She sucked and kissed the mushroom head of his cock making it swell and then swirled her tongue around the head, down his shaft and to his balls. Her right hand came away from his hip and began stroking the shaft of his cock which was slick with her saliva. She began a pattern of four quick strokes up and down his length, followed by three slow much more deliberate strokes which culminated with her rubbing her thumb across the sensitive head of his cock, smearing his precum over the tip of its bulbous head.

"I'm going to take you again, just relax and enjoy and don't fight it. I need this as much as you." Again both her hands went to his hips. She looked directly up at him staring into his eyes before she took him. Her mouth was hot and wet and so, so, soft. The shaft began to slide toward her throat, but this time didn't stop when the head reached the back. Instead it smoothly went into her throat pause only momentarily when she seemed to gag for a second. With consistent pressure she continued to push and push as his shaft went further down her throat. Finally her nose smushed up against his pubic hair, she opened her mouth wide and part of his scrotum went in her mouth. She had done it; she had swallowed all of his cock. The felling was absolutely amazing, incredible, and marvellous so unbelievable he had no words. She held her self there for a short time letting her throat relax and then pulled off of him.

"I want to do that again!" She gasped as she released his cock from her pleasure hold. "I want to do that again and when you cum don't pull out just cum. Don't even fucking tell me just use my throat."

Tony couldn't believe that this was his wife. She was like some sexually charged creature that was exuding sensuality and lust. Again she began the ritual of licking and sucking his cock, kissing the length of his shaft as she stroked him up and down. Several times she rubbed her thumb across the head as she stared at his cock like it was something she had never seen before. She was enthralled by what she was doing and experiencing. Part of her was proud of her ability to take his cock so completely and another part of her wanted a bigger cock, a different cock, one that would choke and gag her like no other.

Her head was again between his legs and her mouth was encompassing his entire shaft. Up and down she slid on his cock taking down her throat. Her speed increased and she became more adept she added new things, little twists and turns to elicit greater pleasure from her partner. Her tongue slid and twisted along his shaft, her teeth nibbled and bit gently. Her throat opened and expanded to accommodate his size and length. Soon she reached out for his hands and placed them on her head so that he could hold her while she sucked him and gave him pleasure. When that was enough for her she began to direct him more, having him push and pull her head up and down his length, faster and harder. She set the speed for him showing him just how rough he could be, she wouldn't break she could take it, she was an experienced whore.

"Oh fuck, oh god." Tony moaned as his cock experienced things he'd never imagined. "That's it, take me, take me bitch. Fucking take all I got. Fuck I love you."

And then it happened he could take no more he was going to cum. His cock got more rigid than it had been and began to swell. Tony began to hump his hips into her face. Rachel's right hand was stuffed down her pants and making exaggerated circles between her legs. Her left hand was at his hips helping her stay stable. When she felt his cock head expand and flex she shoved forward, taking his cock past her gag reflex and into her throat. She could feel him flexing, felt his testicles tightening against her chin and knew he was going to cum. At that precise moment she shoved three of her fingers deep into her snatch as far as they could go and pressed hard against her clit. Tony shot off like a rocket spurting rope after rope down her throat.

"Ahhh. FFuuuuck!" He cried as he shoved his hips forward.

Rachel too let out a guttural sound that was partly stifled by the cock in her mouth as she came. The feeling of the cum going down her throat and the knowledge that her husband was throat fucking her without a care made everyone of her whorish fantasies feel more vibrant and alive. She swallowed everything he had until his shaft quit pulsating in her mouth. She was gently massaging his balls as she slowly, achingly removed his flaccid cock from her mouth. She kissed and sucked him gently continuing to stroke him in her hand as she stood up. When they were face to face he grabbed her head and forcefully brought her mouth to his kissing her and tasting his own cum in her mouth. He loved it and was now lost to her. She was the most sluttish, sexiest thing he had ever seen and she allowed him to fuck her, he couldn't be more lucky.

As she gently pulled away from him she said. "Ok baby how bout we go clean up and you go make supper. You're barbecuing."

He looked at exhausted and befuddled. "Oh, ok well uh fuck, I guess I'm barbecuing"

Supper was good. The family all liked BBQ, most of all Tony. Rachel did the dishes while Tony put things away, it was nice.

"Why are we doing the dishes? Isn't that why we decided to have kids?" Tony commented sarcastically.

"Kid." Rachel corrected "And since your decision at forty was to get a vasectomy it's going to stay that way. Besides I gave him the night off."

In actuality Rachel was feeling somewhat ill-at-ease around Michael after this afternoon's incident and felt distance was the more appropriate response here. "Besides I thought we could share a glass of wine and talk."

Tony wasn't sure how to respond to that. It was so close to the 'We need to talk' line that usually came with the 'Ok I fucked up' feeling he didn't know where to go. Was this in response to the vasectomy that was two years ago.

"I was just tired of condoms and birth control or the worry and panic that came when you were late a couple of times." He stated, "Besides we're going to be 'Empty Nesters' soon."

"Relax baby you're not in trouble."

"Good." You could almost feel the sigh of relief that came with that declaration.

"I thought maybe you'd like to talk about last night."

'Fuck' he thought to himself, I was that far from being scot free. "Um, what is there uh, to uhm talk about really? I liked last night didn't you?"

"Yes I liked last night very much. So much so I showed you how much I liked it this morning. That is I actually let you feel how much I liked it." She had the most devilish smile on her face as she handed him his glass of wine. It was a Zinfandel, blush, not too dry. She was by no means a wine snob, she liked what she liked. A fruity flavour not overly sweet and with a nice aroma.

"So what do you think?"

"The wine? I like it. You've bought this before."

"Not the wine silly. You know what we're talking about."

"Where's Michael?"

"Upstairs and then he's going out. He said something about meeting up with Ronnie Allen."

"Didn't those two get into a fight?"

"That was three years ago."

"Seems to me Michael broke his nose. What the hell was that about again?"

"Some girl. Are you just trying to avoid talking tonight?"

"No." He replied looking at his glass of wine. Caught.

"Well what did you learn?"

"You like it rough?"

"Sometimes." She smiled at him. Again that mischievous look was in her eye. "You want me to be fucked by a rather large cock?"

"Uh, yeah sorta." He was blushing now, looking rather sheepish. Rather similar to how his son was not three hours ago.

"Sorta?" She pried.

"Ok, yeah I do." He countered. "You like dirty talk and nasty names."

"Yeah, a lot actually." That smile just wouldn't go away. "I like being loud and open about what is turning me on."

"You're kinda directive with it."

"Why whatever do you mean?" She replied, feigning innocence.

"Well you go beyond the 'that feels nice' and head full steam into the 'do more that, right there, harder, now do this' talk."

"Well a girl likes what a girl likes, what can I say." She was beautiful and exotic in this moment and it was turning him on completely.

"Apparently a lot when the mood strikes you." They both began to laugh at that last statement.

"So where do we go from here?" Rachel asked feeling a little guarded as it was her that had opened this door for the couple. She was worried about backlash from Tony as he had been very embarrassed about some of his desires. Now that they were out in the open he might just close himself off completely and she didn't want that at all.

"I don't know why?" Tony responded this was all new to him and he already felt exposed with what he had revealed about himself. He wasn't too sure where to go; if she wanted to put it all away he was willing to do so. He also knew that there was more stuff he wanted to explore he just couldn't bring himself to say it; hell what he had already brought up was hard enough.

"Well do we need ground rules?"

"Like?" He was open to anything but clearly was looking to her for direction.

"Well, I don't know. Are there any subjects that are taboo? Too sensitive, too out there for you?"

"As long it's with you I'm willing to try anything."

"Ok I can live with that?" Her smile return with a vengeance and the gleam in her eye struck him.

"So tell me are Sunday nights our only night to play?" He was being bold now and opening the door.

"Not if you don't want them to be? Why what did you have in mind?"

"Well this is all new to me and to be honest I would like to follow your lead."

"You mean to tell me the man that spread my legs apart and threw a fuck into me at three in the morning has no idea what he wants to do?"

"Well I didn't mean that exactly."

"Well what do you mean baby?" God she was playing with him and he knew it, for that matter so did she. He was embarrassed that's what he meant but he didn't know how to say. He was the man after all and he should take the lead but when some of your thoughts and ideas seem a little out there even to you, it's hard to state them without a little motivation or at the very least stimulation.

"I'm not as good at this as you are. I mean I know what I want to say but I can't move into it as quickly as you can."

"Oh so you need a little help getting started then?"

"Yes." He smiled back at her.

"Well then. Why didn't you say so tiger? I'm just the girl to get things going."

"I thought I did?" There was that smile of hers again god what was he getting himself into.

Again the sex was good. In fact it was better than it had been in awhile with the exception of the previous night. Both partners had amazing orgasms and both really enjoyed experiencing their partner in a different way. This night was tamer than the previous night but still held magic and revitalized their appreciation for one and other sexually.

"So how about Thursday night we plan for something special." Rachel spoke after they were done and were lying beside each other staring at the ceiling basking in the afterglow of their sex.

"Special? What do you mean?"

"Well I've had thoughts and plans for awhile know and would like to maybe spring some of them on you. And since I don't have to go in until noon on Friday I thought it'd be a good time to experiment."

"Experiment? Well ok as long as I'm not a complete guinea pig I'll try anything once." He said nervously. Looking up at the ceiling he began to let his mind wander. He was curious as to what she had in mind. "Ok. Thursday works for me, I have a late night Friday with work. Those Japanese clients are coming Friday at three, so we have a four o'clock presntation, dinner and drinks, set them up in the hotel and then two big proposals Saturday Morning. Then they fly out Sunday evening. So I won't be home until after eleven Friday and back out Saturday morning."

"Why don't you stay in town Friday and come back Saturday afternoon?"

"Well that does make more sense, I'll just be missing you that's all." That was legitimately true, he would miss her. He never did like being away from home and the six or seven times he had gone away on business, half the time he found a way to bring her along.

"That way I can give you a special send off and a welcome home party." She smiled at him, batting her eyes playfully.

He chuckled at her silliness, "I can hardly wait."

"Oh, you'll like this I think. Especially if I lace it with some of Sunday nights nasty undertones. You'll like it a lot."

"What do you have in mind?"

"I'm not telling you'll have to wait. Now let's get some sleep, I have a big day tomorrow and planning to do."

They kissed gently for a few minutes and then spooned each other until they fell asleep.

Chapter 3
What's behind the door little girl or Unleash the dogs of war.

Finally it was Thursday and Tony was absolutely beside himself. Rachel and he hadn't had sex for the last two days, they were actually really busy. The point was he was horny. Horny like high school horny, it was all he could do to keep his hands of his wife before, during and after supper. They were cleaning up dishes, Michael had helped. He wanted to go out for the night and was hoping on having a late night if all things went well. The best was to assure that was to help around the house doing whatever little extras needed to be done. He knew that his parents would see him for the suck up he was but that had never hurt in the past. So helping with chores either way was a good idea.

Tony came walking out of into the kitchen after taking the garbage to the garage, when he found his wife alone and waiting for him. She was holding a bottle of wine, the same as they had had Monday night.

"Ok tiger here's what we'll do. We'll have a little wine, not too much. We'll wait for Michael to leave for his friends, he won't be back until late, and he doesn't have practice tomorrow as its Thursday. Then you'll go take a shower in the downstairs bathroom while I freshen up in ours. Then when you're done you meet me in our bedroom. Got it?"

"Sounds good to me. Is there anything else?"

"Oh yeah." She smiled a devilish smile, "shave."

"I already did?" Tony retorted.

"No baby your face is fine, it's not your face I want you to worry about." With that she deliberately reached out and firmly grabbed Tony's groin feeling around until she firmly held his cock in her hand, through his pants, and stroked him firmly once then twice and patted his balls. "You get the picture babe. Turnabout is fair play after all. Oh and while you're at it you could touch up that face of yours, I don't need any whisker burn on my delicate parts.

Michael left and headed for Ronnie's again, this was the third time his week. He'd told his mother he'd probably be back by Midnight unless he'd stay over at Paul's. Either way he'd call and let her know.

Tony took his cue from Rachel and headed for the downstairs shower, toothbrush, toothpaste, razor and shaving cream in hand.

"Leave the stuff in the front there we can trim that down later but the sides, shaft, change purse and taint need to be clean. I can help you if you want?"

Tony couldn't believe what he was hearing she was so bold and forthright. God she was sexy. "Uh no thanks I'm a little nervous as it is and don't need to be any jumpier."

"I promise I'd be gentle. Remember I've had more practice at that than you have." She smiled, waiting for the implication of what she had just said to sink in.

"Hey! Practice, when have you had practice shaving other... Oh yeah, I get it on you. Funny, funny, ha ha."

After he got out, he and put his pyjama bottoms on he went to their room and found the door locked.

"Rachel?" He inquired. And not getting an immediate answer knocked and called out again. "Rachel? Hun?"

"Tony is that you?" Her voice sounded a different somehow but he couldn't place it.

"Ah, yeah. Can I come in?"

"Uhm... Uh... Ahhh..." Her voice tones sounded aroused. "Could you go, ooohhh watch some uh... uh... uh...TV for a minute. Maybe a half an hour or sooo. My lover and I aren't quite finished. Ahh... Ohhh... mmm... Ok just thirty minutes more babe. Please?"

"Honey? Rachel, what's going on in there?" He was feeling on edge. He knew she didn't have anyone in there, at least he thought she didn't.

"Tony. Go watch TV and I'll call you when I'm done. Correction when we're done. Sorry about that lover." The last part almost sounded like she was talking to someone else.

"Rachel?"

"Tony! Go watch TV! I mean it. I love you now go!"

"Ok. I'm going." He stayed a minute and listened a bit longer. Then left to watch TV as he was instructed. This must be part of the role play he thought. He felt odd about it though. Part frustrated and part aroused. He couldn't figure out what she was doing in there and then he decided to go with it. He imagined her in their room with a lover. They were having sex and he was waiting out here in the living room until they were done.

They were doing more than just having sex they were fucking. She and her lover were fucking. Her tight, shaved pussy was being fucked and stretched by a big hard cock. She was screwing her lover in his bed, their matrimonial bed and her lover would spill his seed into her. She would fuck and suck some guys big strange cock, ride him and make him cum without using protection and then when he was done using her, he'd give her back.

The TV was on but Tony couldn't focus on the show. He really didn't know what channel he was watching. All he could imagine was Rachel, whoring herself out, moaning and groaning as she was fucked by a magnificently big cock. God Tony thought I'm becoming one sick puppy. Fuck I want to fuck her so bad right now. His cock and balls were aching. He dared not touch himself for fear he'd mess the couch.

When the show was over, he began to watch the next one, just to make sure she had enough time. You know to get her 'lover' out of the house. He then turned off the TV and went to his bedroom.

Again he found the door was shut and rather than walk in he decided he would gently knocked and quietly called out her name, "Rachel?"

He waited and heard her softly call out, "Lover?"

"It's me Tony."

"Oh." There was a slight disappointment in her voice and a bit of a pause before she spoke again, "Come on in hun, the door's not locked."

The sight before him overwhelmed his senses. Visually there was so much to take in all at once. The room looked to be in disarray, Rachel's clothes strewn about her shoes, nylons, blouse and skirt. All thrown around the room her bra and panties at the foot of the bed. Her panties though, there was something odd about her panties. He looked closer, only to discover they were ripped apart at the crotch, torn open. The room smelt of sex. His wife's sent was everywhere, it flooded his senses. The bed was totally dishevelled. The comforter was on the ground, along with the blanket. The sheet was wrapped around Rachel's lower body. Her legs were uncovered but her hips and pelvis weren't. With the exception of her breast, her chest, shoulders, and arms were exposed to the open air. Her head was propped up on a pillow and her hair was a mess. Her mascara and eyeliner had run, making her look rather like a racoon from all the black around her eyes. Her lipstick was smudge and her mouth looked raw. If he didn't know better he would have sworn someone had been in this room with her. Her legs were spread apart and there was something on both her ankles. She appeared to have what looked like leather cuffs bound to her ankles with silver clasps. The clasps were secured to 'D' rings fastened to long nylon straps, each of which travelled down to the foot of the bed and were attached to the left and right leg of the bed. Her legs were outstretched and opened wide allowing complete access to her sex. She was not quite spread eagled but there was no way she could close her legs. Her arms were stretched out as well. She had the same leather cuffs on her wrists holding her arms apart in relatively same way her legs were. The effect was spectacular, leaving her looking ravished and vulnerable. Yet upon closer inspections you quickly ascertained that she was anything but vulnerable.

Cautiously he approached the bed. "Rachel, are you ok?"

"He just left, you missed him."

"Ok? Who left?" Tony asked not quite following.

"He did my lover." She looked straight up at the ceiling as she spoke and then directly into her husband's eyes, the effect was stunning. "He said to thank you for the use of me and left a note for you on the dresser with that leather box."

"Leather box?" Tony looked over on their dresser and sure enough there was a leather box. It was actually quite handsome with an embroidered stitch along the edges and a brass clasp that held it shut. Tony approached the dresser and there on top of the box was a folded piece of paper. He picked it up and read it.

Dear Friend,

Thanks again for the use of this bitch. God she was tight. I appreciate you letting me stretch her out, she can really take a good fucking and once she gets wet she's really into it.

Inside this box you'll find three toys of varying sizes and a vibrating egg. They're pretty self explanatory in their use. I want you to start with the first size and then work your way up. Use the egg vaginally to increase her pleasure and reward her as she progresses. It is my hope you'll have her ready in less than three weeks. Tell her she has to practice using them with you for the next three nights. Starting Thursday she has to take the first one and wear it all day even at work, for a minimum of three hours. She can take it out for two hours but must put it back in for three. She can do this for five days; take one day off and then move on to the next size. In three weeks I want her ready to take cock.

Thanks

BC

Tony put the letter down and opened the box. Inside he found three anal plugs made out of silver metal, each one bigger than the next and a bottle of lube and an egg shape device with a wire attached to leading to some sort of controller with various settings. Everything fit perfectly into cut out sections in the box, even the lube.

"Oh my." He said as he turned to his wife who lay strapped to the bed.

"What? What is it? What did he leave you and what did the note say?"

"He left me some toys to use for my amusement and the note says you have some work to do." Tony was feeling his role now. He knew what to do, how to meet his needs and hers. After they were done he'd ask her how she was able to orchestrate it all, but until then the illusion was perfect and he would play along. She was the slut wife who couldn't get enough and his was the husband who didn't mind pimping her out as long as he got his fun too. Not quite a cuckold but really a Dom, after all that was his personality. He wasn't prepared to take charge, to be the authoritarian but he was a submissive either, he needed the security and comfort of boundaries. "It says you need to develop a new skill set and I'm supposed to aid you in developing them."

"Oh my!" She said with excitement. "It might be nice to learn something new but I don't think there is anything wrong with my current skill set."

Her look became much more seductive. She could make dishevelled look so sexy. "Why don't you come over here and sample some of my skills yourself?"

"From what I can see you've already been well sampled."

"Well let's just say I was merely put to the test. Mind you it's a test I passed with flying colours. Why don't you come over hear and see for yourself."

Tony approached the bed and began to pull back what little of the sheet still covered his wife. "Oh my god"

"Like what you see baby."

"It's so raw and open." Tony uncovered the portion of the sheet that was between her legs. Her sex glistened and was amazingly wet. The bed sheet was soaked beneath her and it looked like what was ever inside her depths had come out soaking the sheet. "You've soaked the bed."

"What can I tell you my lover has a big cock and he had a big load to go with it. You should've seen his cock sliding in and out of me. It looked more like a small arm than a cock." She knew the visual imagery of her words would stir him beyond his limits.

"Are you sore?"

"Only in a good way. Pull the rest of the covers off and tell me if you like what you see." She teased him; she was nervous and excited with anticipatory delight. She had worried that she had gone too far with her added bits of flare. This next reveal was over the top but she clearly wanted him to know how far she would go.

"Oh fuck, that's amazing." Amazing wasn't the word. He had no words to describe what he saw, exotic, erotic, beautifully frightening, all these escaped him in the moment and came rushing to him after he spoke. Both of her delicately beautiful nipples, that stood out proud and erect were clasped tightly between odd shaped silver clamps, with some sort of dangling toggle apparatus. They were also attached to each other by a matching silver chain.

"You like baby?"

"Oh god yes!"

"They're Japanese nipple clamps. My lover likes me to know who's in charge when he's fucking me. If you pull the chain the clamps pinch tighter."

"There simply amazing. Do they hurt?"

"Of course they hurt baby. That's what there for, to clamp onto my nipples and make them tingle while I'm getting my pussy drilled. It reminds me who I belong to while I'm being fucked. I get so wet and horny when that happens. See my pussy baby; it doesn't get like that by itself."

"No it doesn't"

"Isn't that what you wanted baby to have me fucked and used? To have some big cock stretch me and fill me full of cum." As much as she was trying to turn him on, she didn't want to frighten him off.

"Yes." With that single affirmation her worries were relieved.

"Oh baby mommy is so full of cum. He won't wear a condom baby. I tell him it's one of your rules but he just won't do it."

"Of fuck your pussy looks so fucking gorgeous." Tony was on the bed in between Rachel's legs. His eyes wide and staring, taking in everything that was before him. His breathing rushed and ragged. Rachel's inner labia looked red and swollen and were gapped open. He couldn't believe how stretched she looked. The blanket soaked beneath her, the nipple clamps, his sense were over whelmed. His cock was rock hard as he slid the head into the gapping mouth of her vagina and left it there feeling the heat escaping from her opening. "Oh Christ you're so loose!"

Holding his cock in his hand, he gently put the head inside her and moved his prick around in a circle.

"You like that baby you like the feel of my stretched wet pussy, all sloppy and loose after a big hard cock has been in it?"

"Oh god yes. I love the way it feels soft, warm and wet." He was sliding his cock head up and down her sex, between its lips and across the opening to her depths. He began rubbing his cock against her swollen clit, which was hard an exposed as it glistened from under its hood. She arched her back, tightly pulling her restraints the pleasure over taking her.

"It's been fucked hard daddy, it's been fucked hard and it needs to be fucked again." She continued to moan and began driving her hips up to meet her husband's thrusts, while at the same time she was gyrating them in a clockwise motion, moving them around and around grinding her clit against his body. Her feet were firmly planted on the bed with her legs bent at the knees but still held wide apart by the restraints. She had him deep inside her but god, she wanted to wrap her legs around him and draw him into her even more. He had both hands on her thighs as he knelt between her legs sliding his slick cock in and out of her.

"Ah fuck baby, release my legs so I can fuck you better. Please baby let mommy fuck you better."

God the 'Mommy' thing was turning him on. He continued to pump his cock in and out of her, shoving his prick in as deeply as he could, every once in a while bumping against her cervix, the entrance to her womb. He reached down to her right ankle releasing the clasp and then did the same to her left. Immediately she wrapped her legs around him pulling his body close to hers. Tony fell into her with a terrible thrust, the head of his cock hitting the entrance to her womb. Their mouths met and they began to devour each other, lips and tongue smashed together, intertwining with each other. There breathing became more intense. The sounds of their coupling could be heard throughout the house, raw and animalistic.

"Fuck me baby fuck my cock. Fuck me hard like you did him."

"Mommy's been fuck hard by that big cock." Her hips made dramatic gyrations as she tried to pull him further into her body.

"God some day you have to let me watch! I need to watch you get taken. Please baby let me watch. Please!" Tony began to shudder and shake as he drove his cock repeatedly into his wife. His voice trembled with passion and desire, emphasizing his need to see her fucked.

"Okay, baby ok. Mommy will let you watch, it's alright. You're alright. Shhhh, there baby it's ok." She held him tight soothing him as she did, gently kissing his neck, and he continued to slide himself in and out of her. The ferocity of their coupling slowed but the passion was still present. She was attempting to comfort and nurture her husband as he continued to slide his cock in and out of her. He seemed to get quiet and everything was more deliberate. How he held her, how he stroked himself in and out of her, even how he looked at her.

"Yes baby that's it fuck me." She looked directly at him, catching his eyes and letting him know that he was her lover.

"I'm right here baby. Right here." She continued to stare at him as they fucked.

"Where are you lover, tell me where you are?" His eyes were glazed and his jaw was clenched tightly. He was wildly in the throes of passion, fucking the women below him, his wife, his lover.

"You can do it baby, tell me while you fuck me. Tell me where you are baby?"

"Oh god. I can't, I can't hold it. Oh god. Oh fuck." He was going to cum soon. The thoughts and visions going through his head were too overwhelming for him to express.

"Oh that's good baby just like that fuck me with that cock of yours honey. Make me cum baby make me cum." She knew he was too close and that he was going to cum. It was time to bring him back. Make him cum and bring him back to their bed.

"You like you're present baby. You like the toys you get to use on me?" Again she was looking at him waiting for him to acknowledge her.

"Yes." His voice barely understandable as he continued to pump into her.

"You get to fuck me and get my ass all stretched out and ready baby." His eyes widened as she spoke he was so close now he couldn't hold back.

"Momma's ass all stretched and ready so she can be the nasty whore you want. The slut, baby? You still want me to be a slut baby?" She stretched her neck forward and kissed him on the mouth.

"Is that what you want baby? A slut for your bed?"

"Yes." He groaned as he came inside her, filling her with his cum.

They laid quietly for awhile, him on top of her. His breathing heavy and exaggerated at first then becoming more steady and even.

"You didn't cum."

"No, but that's ok this was for you."

"When did you plan all this?"

"It's been in the works for awhile actually."

"Really?"

"Really." I bought the nipple clamps two months ago on a whim. The restraints I picked up last spring when I was at that conference in Utah. And the box I picked last week."

"So you've been planning this for months."

"No, not really. I've wanted to spice things up for a while now but didn't have the guts. Got close a couple of times, but chickened out. Remember when we went to visit your Aunts and were going to stay at the Hilton?"

"Yeah but she wouldn't hear of it."

"Well I'd brought the restraint and had them in the bottom of my suit case."

"No wonder you didn't want to fly."

"Yeah I don't know what I would've done if some security guard had pulled us aside after our bags went through X-ray."

"Probably nothing. I can't believe that it would be a first for them."

"No probably not. Anyway you're Aunt saved you, or should I say me."

"Well that would've made the visit a whole lot more fun."

"They'd have never seen us." She laughed.

"Probably not."

"Uhm, if it's not too much to ask could you release my arms they're getting sore."

"Sure babe."

Chapter 4
Who's that knocking at my window or what the hell is a camel toe slide anyway.

Michael came home from Ronnie's early. He'd left when Paul had left. Paul had to work in the morning so there was no crashing at his place for the night. It was too bad too as the last time he had slept over Paul's sister, Jessica and he had made out. She was going into her second year of University and was home for the summer. She was smoking hot too. They had hung around the pool that night drinking rum and cokes and doing shots of tequila. That girl could stand on her own. She was wearing this outrageous bikini and was just driving all the guys crazy. All except her brother of course who was a little annoyed at her presence. Anyway she was drunk, he was drunk, there was music and they were dancing or should he say she was grinding on him like nobody's business when he began to get hard. So here he was thinking 'Oh man this is so uncool' when all of a sudden she walked him over to a somewhat secluded part of the back yard and shoved her hands down his swim suit.

"Oh my god Mikey what have we got here?" she firmly had he hand on his cock and began stroking it.

"I don't know what do you think it is?" He replied a little drunk and cocky.

"I think this is the kind of thing that could get a girl like me in trouble, or at the very least knock up. Fuck Mikey you're huge."

"Keep it up it gets bigger."

"Oh my fucking god. Kiss me."

And that's exactly what they did for a good half an hour before people were looking for them and yelling for them to do more shots. The kissed and suck each other's lips, tongues and mouths. Their hands roam and stroked each other. Her hand was smeared wet with his precum. Michael held her firm tits in his hands gently twisting and tugging her nipples.

"Oh fuck Mikey we need to get back." Jessica moaned into his mouth.

"If you say so?" He replied with just a hint of disappointment.

"If I say so. Fuck if I was on my period little boy, there wouldn't be any say so there'd be fucking and sucking and I don't care what else."

"You could suck me now if you like." Michael grinned while they kissed.

"If I suck you, I fuck you and I'm just too drunk to deal with the mess baby." She kissed him one last time as she pushed herself away from him. It took everything she had not to pull his shorts down and fuck him on the back lawn.

And that was how the night was left. She got amazingly drunk and ended up crashing, in her room alone. Paul ended up throwing up all over the back yard. How they kept him from puking in the pool was anybody's guess. Michael and Rob ended up carrying his drunk ass back in to the house when he was finally finished. All the while he was looking at Michael, saying in a drunken slur. "Youah, wanttsh to fucks my sister ya bastard."

"Yeah Paul and your mother too. Now let's get your drunken ass to bed before you fall in the fucking pool and drown your sorry ass." Rob replied and he and Michael carried him down stairs to his room. They all crashed together down there in the basement. Both he and Michael had turned their basements into small apartments with all the necessities a teenager could want; TV, fridge, microwave, coffee maker, and shower. All through the night Michael couldn't keep his mind off Jessica, he kept thinking over and over again 'if only she wasn't my best friend's sister.'

So with no chance of a repeat performance of last week Michael came home.

Upon entering the house the first thing he noticed was that no one had left a light on for him. He found that kind of usual as his mom always left the light on in the foyer on for him when was out and usually the kitchen light was on as well. Bashing his shin on the bench in the hallway he walked around in the dark, fumbling as he went. He made it through the living room and into the kitchen without further injury. As he went to the fridge he thought he could hear voices. Getting a pop from the fridge he headed to the basement, where his room was. As he descended the stairs the voices got louder and he knew they were coming from his parent's room. He stopped in the stairway to listen. Something about how the house was built made the stairway to the basement the most acoustically advantages place in the home. From this vantage point you could hear everything that went on in the house, almost as though you were right there.

"Ah fuck baby I don't think I can do it." That was distinctly his mother's voice and it was clearly in a heighten emotional state.

"Yes you can baby. You took the first one no problem, we should at least try the second." That was his dad.

"Maybe if you put more lube on it. Fuck it's so tight in my ass already." Oh my god they were at it again. This week had been crazy. First of all it wasn't Sunday and by his recollection they had already had sex twice this week and now they were at it again only this time they were working on her ass. What the hell had gotten into them?

"How much do you have in?" He could hear nervousness to his mother's voice.

"About three quarters. I'm going to turn on the vibe and see if that helps."

"Ohh... Fuuckk! Oh my god." Her voice became shrill.

"Here let me turn it up and we'll try to get more in you."

"AAaahhh... You're going to make me cum. Fuck baby. Fuck!" His mother's voice was really loud now and it was very edgy almost like it was going to crack. Michael had never heard anything like it.

"Ok, ok. I'll slow it down and we'll go back to the first one. Ok?"

There was silence for awhile and then finally Michael heard his mother's voice. "Ahhh, yesss... Uhmmm... that's more like it. Ohhh... Fuck... I can do thissss, finger my clit baby. Uhmmm... Kiss me and finger my clit."

The moans of his mother's voice permeated the staircase. Michael couldn't believe how horny he was getting listening to his parents fuck. 'What kind of sick perv am I?" He thought listening to the passionate sounds of his mother as she was getting laid. His cock began to ache in his shorts and he needed to release it or it would explode. It had been months since he'd gotten laid and last week with Paul's sister didn't help relieve any of his frustrations. So intent was he, on making out every word that escaped his mother's mouth that before he knew it he was vigorously stroking his erection while sitting on the stairs. His shorts and underwear were around his ankles and he was so horny he didn't pay attention to his footing. That's when the worst happened. He lost his footing as he shifted his weight to get more comfortable and fell down three quarters of a flight of stairs.

The noise was horrific when heard from his parent's room.

"What the fuck was that?" Rachel's voice flew up an octave. Tony froze with one hand pressing and stroking the end of the anal plug that remained visible. The entire conical head was buried deep inside his wife's beautiful ass. In his other hand he held the remote to the vibrating egg that was lodged in her exquisite pussy. "I don't fucking know he said."

"Christ Michael's home, he's heard us." Panic surfaced in Rachel's voice.

"One of us needs to go check on him?" She stated emphatically. She was naked standing up, leaning face first against the wall, arms above her head, back to her husband, legs spread apart. Her body shimmered with the sheen of sweat that comes from the physical exertion of great sex. Tony was behind her naked as well, his left arm wrapped around her, draped across her stomach descending down toward her sex, the finger of his left hand had her labia splayed as he stroked her clit and fingered her hole. In his right hand he held the tiny remote to the vibrating egg that was lodged deeply in his wife's vagina. The crack of her gorgeous ass and her inner thighs glistened from the stream of clear liquid emanating from body. Some of it was from the large amount of lube her husband had used to insert her anal plug, which remained imbedded inside her, but the majority came from her pussy which flowed with the juices of her sexual excitement.

"Well I'm going to be a minute." Tony said looking at his erection which stood proudly and didn't seem to want to dissipate.

"Well someone needs to see to him, he could be hurt." Rachel's was worried.

"Maybe, but if it's me he'll have to wait a second or two I can't exactly walk down there with this sticking out the way it is."

"Jesus! Hand me my housecoat." She said defiantly. Taking it from him she wrapped it around herself. Two major competing instincts conflictingly ran through her. The first was her motherly instinct, the need to take care of, nurture and protect her son. He second was the lust and sexual need that was coursing through her body. She stormed out of the bedroom and went down the hall and was standing at the top of the stairs when she suddenly realized that her ass was still stuffed with her anal plug and that the remote for her vibrating egg was dangling between her legs. No sooner did she begin to feel mortified when all that changed as she saw Michael sprawled out at the bottom of the stair.

"Oh my god, Michael!" Forgetting her modesty, Rachel ran to the bottom of the stairs, no longer concerned about her appearance or what anyone might think, her baby was hurt and she couldn't have that. He was crumpled into a partial ball, almost fatal, laying half against the wall and half along the bottom of the floor.

His shorts were around his ankles and his shirt had ridden up his torso, revealing most of his chest and gloriously muscled stomach. The first thing that struck was how smooth his body was, although he was muscular, he had virtually no body hair. With the exception of a tiny tuff hair at the base of his penis there was no hair anywhere on his body even his testicles were shaved bald. The effect made his cock look ominous as it lay against his stomach. Even flaccid its length was past his belly button and its girth took the breath from her lungs. Rachel had to consciously force her eyes away from it and begin to check her son for injury.

As she began to examine him starting at his legs and working her way up he began to come to. He had no apparent broken bones and there was no blood. There was a small abrasion on his shin that looked sore but the skin wasn't broken. She moved up his body, again consciously avoiding his groin, and examined his torso, arms face and neck.

"Ah Fuck!" He groaned as he began to come out of it. "Oh shit mom! Oh fuck oh Jesus."

Suddenly he recognized where he was, who he was in front of and just how exposed he was. He began to scramble attempting to pull his clothes back on.

"Easy, easy honey. It's ok Michael, relax its ok. Are you alright?"

"Owe. Huh my head hurts." He began touching the back of his head. "Owe fuck."

He winced in pain as he touched the back of his head.

"Here let me see." Rachel began to explore Michael's scalp, looking for injuries. He had a small goose egg forming at the back but no cuts or lacerations. She gently moved his head back and forth examining it further as she did, she unwittingly drove his head down and forward so that he had a clear view of the opening of her housecoat.

"Uhm, Mom... you're naked?" He said calmly, as she continued to move his head to the right and left giving him more than just a cursory inspection.

"I have my housecoat on." She replied obliviously as though his comments meant nothing. They might as well have been discussing the weather; she was preoccupied with the likelihood of a possible injury.

"Well it's not covering up much." He continued almost as a mild protest to her inaccuracy. His mind was taken back to the incident earlier this week when had seen her half undressed.

"Well you shouldn't be looking." Her tone was emphatic.

"Mom??" His voice raised a tone.

"Yes?"

"What's that?" Michael was looking at what appeared to be a tiny plastic rectangular shaped box, with two dials on it, one red and one blue. A tiny thin wire went from the end of the box and traveled out, taking a path that led right to his mother sex. Without wanting to he began to feel excited and was becoming concerned with his possible reaction.

"What's what?" Rachel looked down, following his gaze to see what he might be looking at. She became completely still when she saw it, the rectangular remote that controlled the egg still lodge deep in her vagina. "Oh... That."

"Yeah that." He said lifting his head so he could look his mother in the eyes, their faces inches apart. Michael could smell his mother's breath, it seemed sweet and mystical. There was another scent coming off her that was less sweet but more mysterious. It seemed to affect him differently, profoundly at a level he was used to, especially when dealing with his mother.

How the hell was she going to explain that? She was indeed mortified. Her face flushed red with embarrassment and spread from her cheeks, down her neck and into her upper body and tummy. As always she knew the easiest way to avoid an embarrassing situation was to meet it head on. Take the embarrassment right out of it by eliminating any power it might hold over you.

"Turn your head... Michael! TURN YOUR HEAD." Her voice was firm but controlled. She held her body stiffly and steadied herself physically. Next she braced herself emotionally as she prepared herself for what she was about to do. She reached down between her legs and grabbed a hold of the wire that was connected to the egg. Grasping it firmly she pulled the egg from her sex. There was an unmistakable sucking sound followed by a distinct plop that you could clearly hear as the egg was being removed. There was no hiding it or disguising it, the sound was sensual and sexual. To Michael it was the sexiest sound he had ever heard. He couldn't help but attempt to look as he saw his mom remove the egg from her vagina and place it and the dangling remote into the pocket of her housecoat. He openly stared at the mouth of her sex which at first gapped open and then slowly closed. With the egg came a river of her sexual juices. Her shaved lips looked so erotic and inviting. He could see her swollen clit as it poked out ever so slightly from under its hood. His reaction was more biological than emotional. Physical, visceral, primitive and primeval, his penis became fully erect.

"AHHH, fuuckk I'm going to cum." And cum he did. Without being touched his cock began to spurt ropes of cum all over his chest, neck and down his stomach. Rachel could actually see his balls contract with each wonderfully awesome spurt. Each spurt caused him to moan aloud almost as though they were painful. By the time he was done, eight thick streams of cum, each at least eleven or twelve inches in length lay across his abdomen. His shame and embarrassment at cumming al over himself in front of his mother overwhelmed him. He was flooded with emotions that he could not in the least way describe let alone handle. Quite out of character, he began to sob quietly to himself and covered his face with his left arm. His embarrassment was deep and profound. He had just gotten off looking at his mom. Mind you she was the sexiest women he had ever seen and she had just finished doing the most erotic thing he had ever witnessed, but it was still his mom.

After the second or two it took her to adjust to the overwhelming display of her son's rock hard cock giving up his seed. Rachel immediately recognizing the emotional significance of what just happened to her boy. Her response was to nurture and support him as only a mother could.

"It's ok baby it's ok." She held his head in her arms and began to cradle him, rocking him back and forth as she attempted to sooth and comfort him.

"Shhh... Now, now don't worry you're alright it ok." She kissed his forehead and held him tightly to her breast.

"Oh mom I'm so sorry, I'm so sorry." He continued to sob and attempted to turn his body away from her. Rachel wouldn't have it, she grabbed him firmly and pulled him back, causing her housecoat to blossom open. "I didn't mean to, I didn't..."

She stifled his words again pressing his face into her chest and shushing him. This time his face came into contact with her skin and she could feel the tears on his cheeks as they trailed down her breasts.

"Stop it baby it's ok mommy's got you, mommy's got you." Again she held him tightly rocking him. Her housecoat open, exposing her breasts completely to him. She brought his face up to hers so she could look into his eyes and know that he was alright. It was an accident, one that she foolishly caused. She was beginning to regret her new found sexuality. She didn't want anything bad to happen to her son. Her beautiful loving son, so strong, so masculine, sexually appealing. Oh god she couldn't believe where her mind was going, she had seen his prick twice now and this last time it was as a full and complete erection. She was becoming reckless and wanton. She had to bring herself under control, find something to do and get out of her head.

"Ok honey let's get you cleaned up and get you to bed." She got to her knees and sat before him. She began to help him to sit up. She stroked his hair from his eyes and cupped his face in her hands, leaning forward she gently kissed his brow, his nose and then his lips. She could taste the salt from his tears. "Shhh... Shhh... Its ok baby mommy will make it all better. Shhh."

She quickly assessed what need to take place. Clean him up, get him ready for bed, get him into bed, reassure him everything would be ok between them, sit with him for awhile and then get him to sleep. It was a long list of things but it was doable and it would get her focus on something other than his gorgeous body and sturdy cock.

At that moment Tony appeared at the top of the stairs. "Is everything alright?" "Yes. Yes he's fine he just tripped coming down the stairs and waked his head." Rachel tried to hide the panic in her voice. The last thing she wanted was to try and explain was how her son was covered in his own cum. She put her body in front of Michael's so that his nudity would be obscured.

"Want me to get some ice?" Tony inquired, genuine concern in his voice.

"No, no were alright. I'm just going to help him to bed and sit by him until he's asleep." Michael's eyes were wide open; he looked scared and was now turning pale. For a second she thought he was going to go into shock.

"You're sure that's wise. He just banged his head. Should he go to sleep right away? Maybe he should come up here and lay on the couch?"

"No he's not going to go to sleep right away; I'm going to stay up with him awhile. Everything's alright I'll be back to bed when I'm done."

"Ok so you're sure everything's alright?" Tony knew she was pissed at him; he should've been the one who went to check on the boy. He had just gotten caught up in his own embarrassment and now he was going to pay for his poor decision.

"Yes Tony. Go to bed I'll be up when I'm done." Her tone was stern and sharp. The last thing she needed was for him to come down and add to Michael's embarrassment. Not to mention her own. Christ he sent her down here in the first place. She was starting to get angry at him, no doubt due to her own embarrassment.

That was it she was pissed. Better to not push it now or he would suffer her wrath later and quite probably for a day or two. "Ok well I'm going back to bed. Let me know if you need anything."

"Not now Tony we're alright." She half turned to look up the stairs at him and give him the glare, the one that said you're about six seconds from me killing you and hiding the body. When she looked and could only just see his legs she was grateful, as it likely meant that he really didn't have a good view of them either.

"Ok first things first, we're going to need a cloth to clean you up. You stay here and I'll get one out of your bathroom." She stood up and began to walk towards Michael's bathroom. As she did so Michael began to wipe his face and pull his shorts up.

"Don't do that honey; let's clean you up first ok."

"Ok." He quietly responded.

Rachel went to Michael's bathroom and got a washcloth from the cupboard. She ran it under warm water and rang it out and then returned to where she has left Michael. He was still on his back, somewhat sitting up. His body was turned away from her slightly and his eyes were closed. His breathing had become less laboured and he appeared relaxed. She knelt down beside him and gently wiped the cloth over his face.

"There baby." She said in and hushed voice. "Mommy will make it all better."

After she wiped his face, she began to wash and clean the stick goo from his chest and stomach. She was able to clean most his chest before the cloth became saturated with his fluids. Some of his cum got on her fingers and hand.

"Ok baby mommy has to go rinse out the cloth and I'll be right back. You stay right there. Right there baby, do you hear me?"

Michael nodded as his mother returned to the bathroom. When she was a little way away from him her curiosity got the better of her and she brought the cloth up to her nose taking in his sent. A sudden thrill came over her and her body shuddered. The anal plug buried in her ass began to intensify those shudders and caused her to moan. Like it or not she was getting aroused. Her nipples harder and became like pointed eraser ends. She didn't have the fortitude to remove the plug as she was unsure of what her reaction might be it came out. First of all would it hurt causing her to scream or yell? Or maybe it would be pleasurable causing her to moan loudly. Either way, she would draw attention to herself and that would affect Michael and he was already embarrassed enough for both of them. Besides she was unsure as to how she was going to live this down as it was.

She continued to breathe in the scent of her son's cum as she walked towards the bathroom and then without thinking purely on impulse she stuck out her tongue and tasted his seed.

"Mmmm... Salty." She said out loud.

"What mom?" Michael asked not quite hearing what she said.

"Nothing." She startled, thinking to herself, 'Nothing at all but the fact that your nasty whore mother just tasted you're cum... And liked it!'

As she went into the bathroom she brought the cloth to her mouth again and sucked it, once, twice, three times tasting his semen. She was overpowered with raw emotion. She began sucking it and swallowing it and then sucking and swallowing it again. She had an overwhelming desire to lean up against the wall and finger herself until she came. As she got to the sink she turned on the faucet, with a trembling hand, and before putting the cloth under the water greedily licked and sucked the cloth of all his fluids. 'Fuck what is happening to me' she thought.

Once the cloth was rinsed and rung out she returned to Michael and finished cleaning him up. "Ok let take of these shorts and get you to bed."

She pulled his shorts down and off throwing them to the side. She would put everything in his hamper once she got him in bed. "Ok now the shirt."

She helped him stand up. God he was a lot taller than her up close.

"I'm so sorry mom."

"Shhh. That's enough now. What do you wear to bed baby?"

"Nothing." He answered.

Fuck she found that thrilling. Down here in the basement was this gorgeous hunk of a young man and he slept naked. She had to focus. "Ok here we are."

She pulled back the covers to his bed and he immediately sat. She took hold of his legs and brought them on to the bed, his body turning as she did. She then brought the cover up over his stomach and left it there. He was sitting up eyes cast down face covered in shame. Once settled in bed he let out a terrific sigh and began to shake as if chilled.

"Here let mommy hold you." She said concerned that he may really be going into shock.

"I don't think you should." He responded blankly.

"Nonsense baby it'll be alright. You're shaking." Her concern becoming more apparent.

"No it won't mom." He said sounding somewhat emphatic.

"Why not?" She asked. In response he simply looked down at his crotch. Although covered by his blanket his cock was making an impressive showing. It stood out at an almost forty-five degree angle and was thick and solid as it began to pull the blanket away from his body.

"Oh my." Without even thinking Rachel's hand went to the hard shaft. It was very impressive, hard as a rock and thick, much thicker than her husband's. Subconsciously she began to stroke its length, feeling its weight and girth in her hand. She pulled the blanket back and revealed it fully to the open air. The head went past his belly button; it didn't look like it belonged on a teenager. It was porn star big. She continued to stroke it her right hand her skin to his skin. Michael opened his mouth to say something and that's when it happened. Boundaries had been blurred and in reality crossed but this was it this was there Rubicon. Rachel leaned forward and kissed Michael on the mouth. Not a peck, not smooch, a kiss. A terribly passionate kiss that said more in the moment it happened than anything they had said before or would say after. This was the kiss of lovers. Strong, passionate and deep with mouths open and tongues touching. Small nibbles and bites and sucking, followed by moans of lust and love.

"Baby can mommy help you with this?" She said as she broke the kiss and looked down between his legs. "Please baby can mommy help you?"

She continued to stroke his shaft up and down the complete length. She stroked him slowly at first and then with greater speed and firmness, her hand unable to contain his width. As she approached the head her thumb ran over the tip, smearing the precum that began to gather there. His head went back and his mouth opened as he let out a gasp of pleasure.

"Can I?" She again inquired.

"Uhh... Oh ok. Yes. Yes." He answered in huffs, his eyes glazed and distant. His mouth remained open.

She leaned forward and kissed him again, taking his lips into her mouth. Her tongue went out into his mouth and sought his tongue. He seemed to come alive and his hands came up to either side of her head holding her tight. Her strokes became much more vigorous as she moved higher on the bed.

"Call me mommy baby please. I know you haven't called me that in a long time but just for tonight. Just this one time. Call me mommy baby." Her voice as urgent as her need.

"Yes mommy. Yes." He responded his own need growing with every passing moment.

"Mommy's going to do something special now, and you can't tell anyone promise baby." She moved up on the bed and began to straddle his waist.

"Yes mommy." He moaned back into her mouth as they continued to kiss.

"Ok. Mommy is going sit across your tummy just like this baby see." Both her legs were on either side of him. She released his cock and reached the sash that held her housecoat closed. She quickly undid it and let it fall open, exposing her naked body completely. Once undone her full firm breasts came into view, followed by her stomach which was nicely defined and only slightly rounded, giving her an utterly feminine look. "I'm not too heavy for you am I?"

"No mommy. No."

"Ok baby now to do this you have to promise mommy you will sit perfectly still and not to do anything mommy doesn't tell you to." She moved forward along his hips until her sex rested against his cock. "Can you do that baby?"

He nodded, his voice failing him as he felt the heat from his mother's sex against his cock. Her labia began to envelop his shaft, one beautifully delicate lip on either side of his cock.

"Ok baby, this is called a camel toe slide." She began to shift her weight up and slide her pussy back and forth along his length, coating his cock with the juice of her sex. "We can't have sex but we can get close, if you can be a good boy."

"You like that?" She asked. How could he not, she was exquisite. Her hips were full and sensual, the kind that were meant for fucking. Her sex was shaved bald with the exception of her tiny little landing strip. He could see the lips of her cunt as they ran up and down his length. Her breast remained high on her torso and her nipples stood out hard like eraser tips.

"You're so hard." She said as she looked deep into his eyes. "Now mommy's going to rub against you head baby and you mustn't move."

She leaned forward putting her arms out straight on either side of his head bracing herself against the wall as she slid up and down his great cock.

"Feel that, feel how wet mommy is? That's cause she's excited baby, she horny." His cock felt amazing to her. He was thick and rigid; it was like riding a rail of hot slippery steel.

Up and down she went from the bottom to the top, she could feel his balls tighten below her and knew she could make him cum again at any point she wanted.

"Ok mommy's going to slide over your head again and stay there a minute. Promise me you won't move." He nodded as she moved forward along his cock, her lips leaking her fluids all over his length. Her clit rubbed against him making both of them moan in illicit pleasure. Once she was at his tip she held her pussy there and moved in gently circles as she pressed down against him. The head of his cock felt as though it had sunk into her part way and was being swallowed in velvet warmth that sent jolts of electric shocks down his shaft to his ever aching balls.

"That baby is the opening to my vagina. That is where you came from." The feeling was amazing, hot wet liquid sex. He had been laid before, a total of six times but nothing he had ever done felt remotely like this.

"Mommy's just going to rock back and forth right here for a little while. You ok with that?" Rachel held the tip of his cock at the mouth of her pussy, rocking back and forth just as she said she would. Pushing down ever so slightly she caused the opening of her sex to suck onto the head of his cock, pulling it into her center. The effect was extraordinary for both of them, she knew he wouldn't complain. Michael placed both his hands on either side of his mother's hips, feeling the sensual motion she was making as she rode along his cock, sliding it back and forth between the sopping mouth of her cunt. He instinctively began to thrust his hips in time to his mother's movements as she rode him. The hot liquid of her sex, soft and slick against his cock. His rock hard prick wanting to drive up, into her opening, and deeply pierce her until it met her womb. This caused his mother to freeze instantly as the pleasure of his attempt overwhelmed them both. She paused and held him still on the precipice.

"No baby you can't. Baby mustn't go in mommy. If baby puts his big cock in mommy, mommy will be ruined." Rachel stopped her movements and held herself still on his raging stiff prick. His erection throbbing and pulsing, in an attempt to lodge itself deep inside her, to make her his body and soul.

"I would never hurt you mommy. Never, I promise." He sounded desperate as he spoke.

"No baby not in a bad way, no. You'll ruin me for others." She sat up and let his hard cock spring forward, standing proud and erect between them. Placing both hands on his chest, balancing herself on top of him, she stared deeply into his eyes. It took all of her self-control not to continue moving. "You have a very big cock baby not many boys have a cock like yours."

She bent over, bringing her face close to his and kissed him. He laid there almost frozen as she did, not sure what was expected or what was allowed. "Aaah fuck... not many men do either." She groaned.

She continued the kiss, gently sucking his lips.

"Touch me." It was a direct but simple request, followed by her placing both his hands on her breasts. At first she held his hands manipulating them to hold and squeeze each tit. She centered each hand over her nipples, manoeuvring his thumbs and forefingers so that they began pinch and pull slightly. "That's it baby they won't break, I pull them harder than that."

She released his hands and continued kissing him. She ran her hands over his chest and began twisting and pulling his nipples. "Touch me more baby, touch me more."

Now he began to run his hands all over his mother. Over her breasts, down her sides to her hips, over her tight stomach and down to her sex, touching her tiny patch of pubic hair. There were two places he was almost too nervous to touch the first was her clit, which he was dying to feel between his fingers and the second was her anus. Slowly and deliberately his hand moved down her stomach loving the feel of the almost imperceptible roundness of her belly. Women were supposed to have curves. He came to the valley of her hips and slid his hand over her Venus Mons, following the trail, the thin strip hair lead to. Placing his thumb over the split that defined her outer labia, he gently pressed and found her clit. The cry of pleasure this elicited from her threatened to echo through the house.

Immediately she resumed her gyrations, sliding up and down his cock with what seemed greater purpose. As her son continued to press against the hard piece of flesh that was her sensitive clit she found herself automatically raising her hips to give him access. As if in perfect response Michael slipped one then two fingers inside his mother feeling her inner depths. The heat was intense and his mind reeled at what he was doing. His heart began to pound, threatening to explode through his chest. His mother's movements became much more pronounces and exaggerated; she was humping his hand like a cock.

"Michael stop. Fuck, fuck Michael, stop! Oh god you have to stop. Michael we can't fuck. I'll do anything you want but we can't fuck." She was on the verge of cumming on his hand and in that momentary moment of weakness would have shoved her son's deep within her belly, giving him what no mother should. "You can't go in baby you can't go in." She said as she lowered her head, wishing it could be different.

She immediately took both his hands in her and placed them on the round globes of her perfect ass. She sat straight up, squeezing him tightly with her thighs, fighting the waves of pleasure that spoke of her pending orgasm. This caused her tits to jut straight out from her body, sitting high and proud on her chest, their nipples poking out, hard as diamonds; you could've hung your hat on them. She took a deep breath.

"Ok, we both need to cum and you need to go to bed, hear me?"

Michael smiled a devilish smile into his mother's face. His hands travelled further down her luxurious ass, gripping it firmly. God he loved the feel of her. He began to trace the crack of her ass with his finger, up and down ever so lightly until he came to her anus and stopped.

"Mommy what's that?" He asked, his forefinger gently touching a round metal protrusion poking out of his mother's beautifully tight anus.

"What is what baby?" She asked. She was still trying to recover from the manipulations he had done to her clit and cunny. God she had almost let him fuck her.

"That right there at your bum." Michael pressed the metal nub, pushing whatever it was just that much more into her rectum. The response was equally as amazing as when he had rubbed her clit and fingered her pussy. Her whole body shock on top of him and she bit her lip as her eyes rolled into the back of her head. Again she squeezed his thighs tightly trying to ebb the flow of energy that would set her off.

"Mommy was hoping you wouldn't notice that." She shuddered again as he continued to push and swivel the little nub, having no idea just how big the plug was that was stuffed up her ass. If he had maybe he would have been a little less forceful.

"Well mom what is it?" He asked, his tone changed and he sounded a little more commanding. He firmly pushed this time causing his mom to groan with pleasure and then sigh deeply, after which she opened her eyes and stared at him hard.

"It's mommy baby, remember? You must call me mommy or the fun ends." She had to get back in control or this whole thing could end up nasty. And at this point, as fucked up as things were, she was sure there was no coming back from her son seeing her get nasty.

"Ok mommy. What is that thing sticking out of my mommy's ass?" He said straight out.

"Oh how forceful. Well baby if you must know. It's an anal plug or butt plug." Rachel's voice changed. Gone was the gentle mommy voice and here was the dominant women's voice. The Bitch that knew what she wanted and took it.

"It's used to stretch my ass and make it ready for cock. And not just any cock. Big hard cock that knows what its doing and can pleasure a woman. A hard cock that can throw a fuck into me and not leave me wanting. You know that type of cock little man? Have you seen that type of cock?" Her voice was hard and intimidating. She ground her sex into his cock deliberately almost to the point of causing him pain. His eyes got big as saucers and he was suddenly very aware of his surroundings.

"Sorry mom. Sorry." He apologized. God he was doing that a lot lately, he really needed to stop.

"That's alright. Now are we done with all the questioning of your mommy? Can you behave and can we finish what we started?" She looked directly into his eyes. She knew things had permanently changed between them, they were going to be lovers, it was just a matter of time. She had honestly hoped otherwise. She had hoped that this was a onetime thing and that both of them would see it as a mistake and hide it away as families sometimes did.

"I'm sorry mom it won't happen again. I'm sorry." Again with the apology a simple yes would've done he corrected himself.

"What are you suppose to call me."

"Mommy. I'm supposed to call you mommy."

"That's better." She continued to slide along his cock; the heat coming from their body's increasing their mutual pleasure. Her son's thick cock splaying her open and helping her to grind her sensitive clit against him. Up and down she traveled getting wetter and wetter as she went. She again began to center herself over his head, careful not to draw him in. His precum adding to their fluids, creating a slick river of liquid. His sensitive head jumping every time she slid over it.

His hands traveled up her waist and to her firm full tits, squeezing and pulling on her nipples as she had shown him. She leaned down to kiss him, their tongues intertwined as she rode him. She loved the feel of him between her legs and wished she could draw him in, but without protection it would be disastrous.

"Oh baby are you close?" She asked as she felt her own orgasm approaching. Her clit hard and protruding from its hood like a tiny little cock, fuck she loved when it got this way. She had to fight the urge to put her hand between her legs to bring herself along as she knew that would only lead to her shoving her son's dazzling cock deep inside her.

"Talk to me honey tell me what you're feeling." She looked down at her son he was glorious, his muscular chest and abs, his narrow waist all drove deeper and deeper into her lust filled haze.

"I want you mom. I want you." He cried out in desperation. He need and desire superseding what was moral, what was right.

"I know you do baby I know you do. I want you too, but we can't." She had to keep her head. She was too far gone as it was and one slip and she would be fucking the boy all night, right into to the morning and probably the next day.

"Please mom please." He moaned.

"Not tonight baby not tonight. Oh fuck." What was she saying she was promising, inferring that there'd be more. Oh god, of course there'd be more how could there not be more. She was lost her lust and love for the boy overwhelmed her and knew she would have him and he would have her.

"Mommy's going to cum on you baby. Mommy's going to cum all over your beautiful cock." Her body took over now, what will she had left was gone, she couldn't fight it, she didn't want to. The wave of pleasure began at her very center, her core and radiated out, like a wave, punctuated with sharp bolts of electricity that made her convulse and shake on top of him.

"Oh, fuck I'm going to cum." And there it was her orgasm, bright and hard and beautifully terrifying all at the same time.

"Me too. Me too!" "Oh fuck. Oh Fuuck!" His cock began to spurt and spurt between the lips of his mother's cunt. All he wanted in that moment was to bury his hard prick deep inside and fill her with his seed. He didn't care that she was his mother, didn't care what others thought or would say. At that moment he was so deeply in love with the woman above him he would die for her, give up his very life to see that no harm came to her, he was lost.

His cum covered his stomach and chest. Four solid ropes, not as much as he'd done earlier but still surprisingly enough. She couldn't help herself, nor did she care. She bent down in one swift motion and sucked and licked every drop of his cum into her mouth, swallowing it as she went.

"Mmmm.... god that was good." She said as she looked up at her son, lick his cum from her lips, her eyes gleaming and her smile brighter than he had ever remember it. "Not a word baby, not a word. You promised."

"I know mom, not a word." He immediately leaned forward and grabbed with both hand bringing her face to his. In a surprise that took both them unexpectedly he kissed her hard. He could taste his cum in her mouth on her lips and he didn't care. He wanted to show her that beyond a shadow of a doubt he loved her and loved what they did, there would be no embarrassment, awkwardness, unease between them.

After the shared kiss his mother collapsed on top of him. They stayed like that for several minutes until their bodies relaxed. Once her breather became regular his mother was the first to move. She reached up and brushed the hair away from her eyes and then stroked his brow as she had done several times in the past. It was a gesture of love and nurturance that she had done forever. She kissed him again, a gentle lovers kiss. A kiss goodbye, a kiss goodnight, a kiss that says I will see you again don't worry my love. Without words she reassured him with those simple gestures that all was well. As crazy things now stood, she still loved him, he was her son and she was his mother and nothing would change that bond.

"Now good night I love you." She said as she gathered her housecoat. She couldn't remember when she had tossed it aside. She stood naked before her son, her lover and didn't cover up, there was no longer any reason to, modesty no longer existed between them, they had seen all there was to see and soon very soon there would be more. Much, much more.

"I love you too mom. I love you too."

When she returned to her room she found Tony asleep in their bed.

"Is everything alright?" He asked.

"No, but it will be." Tony looked at her funny, unsure what to make of what she had just said. She saw that look he was giving her and at moment rather than undergo any question she decided to ask her question first.

"Want a blow job?"

Chapter 5
Once the horse has left the barn, that's not all that won't get back in.

To say the sound was abrasive was an understatement, but at Six Forty-five in the morning anything that disturbed the calm and quiet of the new day could only be described as abrasive. Tony woke up abruptly and attempted to quiet the alarm as it went off. One hand fumbling for the switch while the other covers the speaker, turned out to be more disruptive than had he simply turned the alarm off directly. Friday morning alarm blaring, he had really not wanted to wake Rachel. She didn't have to be up with him as she had arranged to have the morning off from work. But as with all well intended plans it wasn't to be, Tony was unable to turn the alarm off quick enough and of course they were both now up. When he saw that she was awake he apologized. "Sorry babe, I tried not to wake you. If I could get up without an alarm I would."

She looked at him through the fog that came from being up way too late and smiled anyway. "Not your fault hun, you have to work."

"Well, try and go back to sleep I'm just going to hit the shower and be on my way." He said.

"Do you think Michael up?" She asked.

"Probably not he's never up without one of us going down there to get him started. He's more than likely still sleeping." Tony got up and began to get showered and dressed. He selected which of the two suits he was going to wear first and fished the rest of his morning routine. He had picked out shirts and ties last night that went with each of his suits, had ironed everything ahead of time, so that he wouldn't have to iron in the morning, packed his travel case and his overnight bag and put them in the kitchen. Once there he grabbed a coffee, automatic timers were such a great thing, and then returned to their bedroom for one last check to see if he forgot anything.

Rachel was sitting up when he came in the room looking radiant. She was covered only with a sheet and was naked underneath. If he didn't get a move on he'd never leave.

"So, what happened last night anyway?" He asked, referring to Michael's fall down the stairs.

Rachel stretched. One arm holding the sheet to her chest the other held high above her head. "In our rush to have our fun, we didn't leave any lights on. He was just trying to be respectful and not wake us, so he didn't turn on any lights, he slipped and fell down the stairs." The truth of the matter was that she really didn't know what happened. All she did know was that she and her son had broken more boundaries than a mother and son should and as a result their relationship was likely going to change, as new boundaries formed to replace the old.

"Well good thing we heard him before he heard us. That could have been embarrassing." Tony laughed half heartedly unsure if she would find his little joke funny. After all it really should've been him that had checked on the boy. She was in no shape at the time to go traipsing through the house.

"Good thing." She said in return not really sharing her husband's humour. "I'm going to get up and check on him later and then I'm going back to bed, I may take the whole day instead of half."

"Well you deserve it hun. Remember I'm staying in town tonight so don't have supper waiting." Tony moved through the bedroom making sure he hadn't forgot anything. He had dressed in one his more professional looking suits, a sharp olive green, that he pulled off so well, with a dark maroon shirt and black tie and dress shoes. Rachel was amazed at how quickly men were able to go from Saturday, Sunday weekend wear you wouldn't clothe a dog in, to a suit and tie, looking as fabulous as the day you married them. "Ok, see you when I get home."

With that he came over as she sat up in the bed, cover only in a sheet, god she looked ravishing, gave her a kiss on the head, grabbed his car keys, lap-top and overnight bag and off he went.

Now that Rachel was up she smelled the coffee in the coffee pot, walked into the kitchen and poured herself a cup. She didn't bother getting dressed, Tony was gone and after last night with her son, her modesty was gone. She put her cup in the sink after she was done, checked the doors to make sure they were lock and head down stairs to her son's bed.

Michael was sound asleep in his bed when she got there. He looked every bit as handsome as he always did but now there was something else. She saw him differently. Now instead of a young boy with stars in his eyes, she saw potential. Not that she hadn't seen potential in him before, but this was different, this wasn't the potential of youth, this was the potential of a vibrant young man. This was her lover.

She approached his bed and pulled the sheets aside. He was naked and his body did things to her that it shouldn't. She got in the bed behind him, causing him to startle and wake.

"Shhh... Everything's alright go back to sleep."

"Where's dad?" He questioned. She could hear the nervousness in his voice; he was caught off guard and apprehensive, good. "He's gone. He won't be back until supper tomorrow. Move over and let me in."

He did and she snuggled up behind him. The affect was instantaneous, his cock became fully erect. She pulled him close to her, he could feel her breasts in his back, her hips and legs and that remarkable little patch of pubic hair against his ass.

She reached across his stomach from behind and took a firm hold of his rock hard penis, she couldn't close her hand around it, it was so thick and that immediately mad her pussy went.

"I know you're horny and so am I, but right now I'm tired and I need some more sleep. So close your eyes and go back to sleep, you can fuck me when we get up."

She kissed the back of his neck and stroked his cock gently while she soothed him with soft kisses and loving whispers. Her hand went up and down his shaft with practiced ease. She came to large head and feeling the precum that began to flow from the tip, she rubbed her thumb across it.

"That's right baby, you're going to fuck me. You're going to put this big beautiful cock inside me as deeply as it can go and fuck me. Are you ready to be mommy's lover baby? Are you ready to take your place between her legs?"

He came in moments. How could he not, she had just answered his prayers as wrong as they may have been. He was relieved, he was in love, total adoration and he was scared he was alone in that. But now she was here, in his bed, reaffirming everything they did last night and more. She said he was her lover and that was all he wanted.

"We'll change the sheets later. Now get some sleep. I love you."

"I love you to mom. Thank you, thank you. I love you so much."

"I know baby, me too. Now get some sleep. You're going to need it."

They slept for another two hours and then their bodies just wouldn't allow them to be apart. Like magnets each was attracted to the other and it was only a matter of time before they were joined.

"God mom you're tight." He groaned, looking at the unbelievable sight of his naked mother. She was on top of him, riding his cock. Her full, firm breast rising high on her chest. Her stomach firm with a slight roundness to it just below her belly button, that all women he age hate but just looks so damn sexy. Her sex was shaved smooth with the exception of a very neatly trimmed rectangle of hair, closely cropped about a half an inch wide and two inches long. She had just engulfed his erection, in what was a slow brutally pleasurable process if ever those two terms could be put together.

"That's because you're a big boy." She breathed out as she spoke. She was straddling his waist; his cock was sliding in and out of her. She was actually naked sitting on top of him, her full firm breast jutting out towards his, her nipples mere inches away from his lips.

"I may cum quickly." He groaned, his brain having difficulty taking in the unbelievable site before him.

"That's ok baby we've got all day and all night." She continued to slide up and down the magnificently large and engorged cock that belonged to her son. The juice of her cunt making the shaft slick and shiny as it deeply penetrated her sex, stretching her vaginal walls and threatening to push through into her cervix on every down stroke.

"Oh fuck mom I can't believe this." He said and then became immediately embarrassed for using the 'F' word. "Oh I'm sorry I didn't mean to swear."

"Yes you did baby it's alright. You are fucking me after all." To show him everything was alright, she leaned forward and placed a kiss on his lips. Quickly this kiss turned passionate as she began to suck his bottom lip into her mouth. This was immediately followed by her tongue entering his mouth and grappling with his own. From the outside it could be said that the two lovers were attempting eat or chew the face off the others partner as the passion began to build in the kiss. When she finally, slowly pulled away from the boy and looked him deeply in the eyes, a slight strand of saliva clinging between both their lips, she licked her lips like the satisfied lioness she was and began to speak.

"Mmmm that's so nice baby. Your big beautiful cock is in so deep." She ground her pelvis into his to emphasize the point. The head of his cock pressed tightly against her cervix again, stretching her in ways she had never dreamed. She had never thought of herself as a size queen but quickly realized that she could easily become one. "You feel that baby. That's mommy's cervix your big beautiful cock is hitting. That's the place you came from. I think your cock wants you to go back there baby, hmmm. What do you think?"

"Oh fuck mom. Fuck." He moaned. He was overwhelmed with emotion the chief of which was desire.

"That's it baby fuck mommy. Fuck mommy's tight, wet pussy. You want to cum in me baby." Her own words were getting her excited.

"You want to cum in mommy. Fill mommy with your cum, with your seed." As soon as she said it the erotic notion of it struck a profound chord within her. Her son would be planting his seed in her. His cum would be in her. His beautiful tight balls would be releasing hundreds if not thousands of little baby making sperm inside her. And sperm doesn't care who you are, wife, lover, and sister, mother their genetic code knows only one thing. Find the egg and impregnate it. God that was raw, powerful, sexy and scary all at the same time.

"Oh fuck mom. Fuck yes; I want to cum in you. I want to cum in you and make you mine." The words coming out of his mother's mouth were driving him crazy, taking him to the edge. There would be no holding back, no delay. He wanted this to last but she was making that impossible.

"That's it baby make mommy yours. Make mommy yours." She leaned forward and began to kiss him again.

This whole time Michael's hands were on her hips feeling the rise and fall of her ass as she fucked him senseless. As she leaned forward her right arm and hand stretched out behind his head to help brace her as they kissed. Her left hand traveled over her left breast, stopping briefly at her nipple to twist and pull it. She pulled the nipple straight out from her body, moaning loudly into her son's mouth as she did so. Her hand then went down her body over stomach and to her sex were two of her fingers pressed her clit into her body to her body. She dug in hard with the two fingers pushing on her clit and messaging it a circular motion at first clock wise than counter clock wise. Again she moaned loudly into Michael's mouth. "Aaaaahhh, Fuck!!"

To Michael's surprise the fingers went from her clit to the opening of her sex and slid in around his cock. First just the two, and then a third and soon, a fourth. She began to grind furiously into him at the same time, her hip sharply pushing forward and back almost painfully trapping her fingers and hand between them. All this time her mouth was attached to his sucking and kissing his lips. Her tongue searching his mouth finding his tongue and duelling with it. Once capturing it she would suck it into her mouth and let it go. Her breathing becoming deep and ragged she would breathe in through her nose and out through her mouth in the fantastic sound hisses of breath. She would pause momentarily resting her forehead against his. Sometimes her eyes would flutter ad unbelievable jolts of pleasure would coursed through her body and other times she would stare deeply into his eyes as she gulp deep amount of air into her lungs staring wildly at him with a mixture of passion and unbridled lust. It was then that she pulled her hand from between their sex and shoved the three fingers soaked with her juices into to his mouth.

"Taste!" She groaned as she shoved the fingers into his mouth. He sucked and licked her finger obligingly until they were clean of her juices. Immediately her hand went back between them and she repeated the grinding ritual and again she withdrew them and said, "Taste!"

On the third occasion she pushed her fingers into her own mouth. "You need to be nastier Michael. If you want to make this bitch yours, you need to be nastier."

She began to ride his cock vigorously now. He knew he was done for, he would be cuming shortly. It was taking all he had just stay with her now.

"I will give you time to learn baby, but you need to be nastier." Again she was looking him straight in the eyes. While she rode him, leaning forward and kissing his mouth and fucked.

"You think you can do it Michael? You think you can fuck me into submission? Can you Michael? Can you?"

Her paced quickened and Michael's head slammed back into his pillow.

"Squeeze my tits. Squeeze my tits and pull on my nipples. Squeeze them, pull on them, bite them."

That was it he couldn't hold it any longer. He began to cum. A torrent semen raced from his balls through his shaft and out. He could feel his prostate gland flex and contract violent and he came. Spurt after spurt, volley after volley his cum surged through his cock and out into his mother's receptive womb.

"That's it baby cum in me. Don't pull out, cum in me. Give mommy your seed baby. That's what you want to do baby. You want to give mommy you seed don't you. That's my boy. Good boy." She began gently kissing him now rubbing his chest as she made circular motions with her hips riding him mashinh their sexes together. Her cunt was stretched and full, her clit pressed firmly against his pubic bone. She moved back and forth, around and around, and then as if by accident she pressed forward grinding herself into his pubic bone in an attempt to extract a last gasp of pleasure from him when it happened. The constant wave of bliss she had been riding broke and surged. Her own orgasm took her by complete surprise. She hadn't expected it and actually didn't think it would happen the first time they fucked. There would be just too much raw energy for the boy to handle she thought. But she was wrong. The wave of pleasure and release seemed to start in two places at once. It radiated out from her centre like a hot aching itch, while at the same time coming from her toes and moving up her feet, through the arch and into her calves and thighs. Her muscles tighten and froze as though her body was in one big glorious cramp. And then, there it was the sudden release and spasmodic convulsion of all her muscles, almost seizure like. She could feel her body blush all over. Her nipples hard and pointing straight out, her breasts flushed with heat that again radiated up her neck into her face causing her ears to burn. She convulsed again with a sharp intake of breath.

"Uhnnnnn!!!! Mmmmm! Ohh, fuck. Fuck. You bastard! Fuck." Another spasm ran through her. She bit her lip. Her arms came forward in front of her, she pressed her hands against his chest to stabilize her body and stop herself from crashing forward. Another spasm and her knees came forward so that she was sitting up more than riding him. He was still lodged inside her, her vaginal muscles had clamped tightly around his cock refusing to let it go. Her body was mating. Regardless what she wanted to call it, fucking, sex, experimentation, her body was calling something else. She was breeding herself on this man beneath her.

Michael didn't know what to do. Nothing in his young life had prepared him for this. He had a good childhood, a great upbringing. He was loved by his parents and in turn he loved them back. There were no huge traumas, no big upsets. So when his mother began crying, uncontrollably sobbing he was at a complete loss.

Her voice was soft and quiet between the sobs and tears. "This wasn't supposed to happen. You weren't supposed to be able to do that to me. Fuck you Michael, fuck you."

"I'm sorry mom. I'm sorry" Was all he could muster. He was confused. She had come to him. She had seduced him. Oh he had wanted it, he had always wanted it but he hadn't started it nor had he set out to hurt her.

"Sorry? Sorry. Oh no son not sorry. My beautiful, beautiful boy there is nothing to be sorry for. Oh god no. I love you. I always have and I always will."

"Then what mom? Why are you crying and why are you calling me names?" He looked straight at her. He had both arms wrapped around her and was holding her ever so close to his chest. He had sat up straight in his bed and was cradling her, very much like she used to cradle him when he was younger.

"No Michael I wasn't calling you names out of anger. I was speaking to you out of love and emotion. I came on you Michael. I came on you harder than I ever have in my entire life baby. Harder and stronger than I have with your father. Harder then when I masturbate, and I do masturbate baby, a lot."

"Is that a bad thing?"

"No baby it's not a bad thing. It's just a thing, a very good thing. A very unplanned and surprising thing. But it's a thing none the less." She said again looking into his knowing he was too young to understand what had just happened between them.

"I know I'm not your first baby, you have had sex before, but has it been or felt like what we just had?" She kept looking at him, her hand gently caressing his skin in an almost absent minded manner.

"No, not quite." He replied. "This was different. More intense, more mind blowing. Mom I just don't have the words."

"That's ok baby I do. What happened, what you did to mommy doesn't happen very often I don't think. I've had good sex before and up until now I thought I'd had great sex but that's not true anymore. In fact I've never had sex like we just had before in my life. Not ever."

"Well you've only had two lovers mom."

With that said Rachel look down for the first time. "What I'm about to tell you doesn't leave this room. Do you understand me?"

There was that Mother Tone he had so grown up with. The tone that told you she was serious and that there was no fooling around. The tone that said don't push me buster or there will be hell to pay and you'll be paying it, I don't care how old you are or how big you'll get I am your mother and you will listen to me and do as you are told DO YOU UNDERSTAND ME. Yeah that tone.

"Twelve years ago your father and I were going through a rough patch. Nothing serious at first all couples go through them but it was hard on your father and he was feeling old and out of touch. So like all men looking at middle age he panicked and got scared. Well instead of turning to me like he should have he turned to someone else. He had an affair. When I found out your dad and I talked it through and he ended it. I was angry and was getting over it when your father suggested that turn about was fair play. He took it upon himself to point out every available guy he could find. At every party we went to at every wedding we attended. He became obsessive. Then one day just so he'd let up I said fine and went on a date. Nothing happened and it was over and your father stopped obsessing. However the bug had hit me and now I wanted to experiment and so I did, twice."

"Oh wow mom and dad doesn't know."

"No and I prefer he didn't. They were awful mistakes on my part. Sure the sex was nice and once was utterly fantastic but there was nothing to the relationships. There was no connection no real bang."

"Ok and you're saying today was different."

"Yes, baby today was different. Today was bang. The stars lit up and my body melted and today was bang baby bang!"

Through this whole conversation Michael's cock remained inside his mother. Although he wasn't as hard as he had been he really didn't go quite soft so when they began to reposition themselves as they talked and his mother kept touching him his cock began to get hard again and throb.

"Baby?"

"Yes, mom." He replied.

"What do you think you are doing?"

"Why whatever do you mean?" He replied.

"When you claim a woman Michael and make her yours. You need to know she won't go elsewhere, unless you tell her."

"So as your Bitch Michael I am asking for one favour and one favour only. After this, after I give myself to you and my body is yours I won't be able to ask you for anything, I'll belong to you Michael do you understand?"

"Yes."

"I need you to let me... No, that's wrong I don't need. I asking that you let me continue to have sex with your father."

With my father? Michael hadn't considered that. He hadn't considered his father. He hadn't really thought it through. The idea that his mother would be his and his alone hadn't occurred to him. The thought that she would belong to him and as such wouldn't be with anyone else didn't quite cross his mind. It turned him on immensely mind you but he really didn't understand the implications but apparently his mother did and that was why she was making this request before they moved forward from here. He wondered what she would say if he said no. Would that be it then, would they never have sex again? Was this the line in the sand?

"What would happen if I said no?" He asked.

"Are you saying no?" She countered. A questioned answered by a question. She was glad he was so young because someone older more experienced wouldn't have tolerated this much they would've simply taken her and that would be it. She held his gaze hoping he didn't push and she wouldn't have to make the choice. It really wasn't a choice though. There was no real decision. She couldn't stay away from him. The door was opened that couldn't be closed and she couldn't fight how she felt. If they didn't answer this question now it would come up again, maybe not the next time they made love but certainly the time after that or the next. Her mind was racing and she was scared. She was now referring to them having sex as making love. She was lost and she knew it, if he pushed she knew what the answer would be. It would be horrible. It would be frightening, but it would be true. She was his and she knew it. She knew in time she would be his and his alone. She would be wrecked and ruined and lost but she didn't care she would be his whether he chose to have her or not, she would be his.

"Ok. Ok then." He said flatly. He looked at her with love and devotion and a hidden sadness for fear of losing her. "Ok, you can still be with dad. But I don't want to know about it. I don't want to hear you two fucking. I don't want to hear you being loud, nothing."

She smiled at him and got a devilish look in her eye. Playful and erotic. "Are you sure you don't want to hear your Bitch being used. Knowing that she is fucking some guy simply because her Master and lover told her to. That her cunt is getting fucked and used because she is after all your slut and your whore, to be used as you see fit. She is your property after all and belongs only to you. Like any piece of property you own you can lend it to your friends as you see fit and the property has no say, it just does what it's told and goes where it sent. If you want you can send it out all clean and shiny or you can send it out all used, stretched out and sloppy. It's totally up to you."

"I never quite thought of it like that, we'll see what my mood brings."

"Now you're getting it baby. Now tell Momma what she can do for you."

"Well you can start by cleaning this sloppy mess you poured all over my crotch, blanket and bed."

"Do you want me to get a cloth or use my mouth and tongue?"

"Oh my."

Chapter 6
Everyone has an Oedipus complex, don't they? or Give it up dad cause mom just did.

Rachel and Michael spent the day in and out of bed. It was like they were different people, communicating on a very different level. They had talked about a number of things that morning, school, work, sports, and life in general. A significant portion of their conversation had been on Michael's choice of University. He had made his decision by comparing both athletic programs and academic opportunities. He wasn't foolish by any means, and knew that the only way to get ahead was through education, sport was a good in but the likelihood of playing professionally was slim. Rachel talked about her university experiences, although they were vastly different than his were going to likely be, she did hers part-time, was married and had, had a kid. It took her six years to do what most kids had done in four but regardless she came away with a degree in Business Administration. It also explained why Michael had no siblings; his parents were busy with their educations and fighting the stigma of being young parents. The conversation meandered through university life, class choices, the importance of studying, to parties, girls, and finally the conversation turned to sex.

"So I take it from your performance today that you're not a virgin?" She had a sly smile on her face as she spoke.

They were back in Michael's room; she was standing across from him, leaning against his desk, sipping from her coffee cup. She was still naked; she had been naked all morning, not bothering to dress because she was still planning on fucking him some more. Her nudity seemed natural, the whole sordid mess seemed natural, erotic and taboo sure but there was no guilt, no crazy emotional outbursts of fear or fright at what took place between them, all in all she felt exhilarated. To put it bluntly she felt like she was a teenager again and she was in love/lust with some hunky guy who if she played her cards right would be fucking her silly for a long time. So being in her son's room naked actually felt quite good, surprisingly. She had her left arm folded across her body just under her breasts, as she continued sipping her coffee, this pose accentuated her firm gorgeous tits which sat high on her chest, and her legs were crossed at the ankles, giving greater emphasis to her hips and thighs. Her beautiful hour glass frame overwhelmed him at times, especially given the view he had of that perfect little landing strip less than an inch wide that lead directly to his mother's tight pouty vaginal lips and heaven. If he bothered to look closer he would have noticed her heightened arousal, starting with the flush of her skin at her neck and breast, how it travelled down her center over the imperceptible curve of her stomach to her groin and her Venus Mons. The blush of her skin radiating out signifying the body's desire for sex and culminating at her vaginal lips that are moistening and becoming wet, indicating her readiness to copulate. But being young and inexperienced he couldn't get past her all over tan that accentuated her shapely look and help to highlight her shaved vaginal area, firm breasts with their silver dollar sized areolas and hard nipples.

"So, what was the question again?" Michael broke from his daydream, shaking his head slightly, causing his eyes to blink and refocus.

"Are you a virgin?" She repeated, smiling as she noted his reverie. It signified to her just how enthralled he was with her and she loved it.

"No, I'm not." Michael blushed again as he answered. He was sitting up in his bed drinking from the water bottle his mother had just handed him. She had come down the stairs from the kitchen naked, handed him the bottle of water, as though her naked appearance was an everyday occurrence. She turned and walked over to his desk, so he could watch that perfect ass of hers sway as she went. The image just kept playing over and over again in his mind, distracting him and making completely unfocused. Her body was toned and well muscled, firm and sexy. She again turned to face him leaning casually against the desk as though it was perfectly natural to be in his room without clothes. He stared at her agape eyes looking glazed over.

"What?" She asked smiling at him knowing full well the effect her nudity was having on him. He was paused staring at her, his facial expression clearly indicating shock and awe.

"I just can't get over the fact that you're naked in my room." He said looking at her.

"Really, I'm naked in your room and that has you flabbergasted; the fact that you just fucked your mother hasn't blown your mind at all?" She continued to smirk, the fact that they had fucked did more than just blow her away, she was euphoric. Deep down she knew that she should be in turmoil, she should have misgivings and pangs of guilt but instead she was remarkably aroused and horny as hell. The sex she had just had with her son was better than anything she had experienced before. When she was upstairs making coffee and getting her son a bottle of water she found her mind wandering back to their time together this morning. She had never considered herself a size queen but after this morning she definitely was considering things differently. The size of his cock stretching her and penetrating her more deeply and thoroughly than anything ever had, push into her cervix wowed her beyond belief. Size wasn't the only thing that shocked her, she found herself turned on by the idea of incest. It added an erotic edge to their love making that she hadn't counted on and her son's staying power was just an added bonus. They had plenty of time before his father came home and she intended to make the most of it.

"Well yeah that has me blown away a bit for sure." He said looking down at his feet and rubbing his hand through his hair. He had always known his mother was hot. He had fought it though not willing to go there; he had even fought with his friends when they brought it up but after bumping into her when he came out of the shower well that changed everything, dramatically. Things were moving fast and he really didn't have time to assess their relationship. Their relationship that fact alone just began to sink in, he and his mother were in a relationship. "I really don't know what to think about that."

She smiled again at him and slowly sipped her coffee, very aware of her body. Her nipples were hard and erect standing out from the roundness of her firm breasts like pink eraser tips. She could feel herself becoming wet and knew she wanted to fuck him again. The question was would he want to fuck her again, she knew he'd likely fuck her again today that much was a given, but would he want to keep this going, would he want something more, would he want a relationship? "Well you'll just have to get used to it because I plan on being this way more often. Is there anything else you're having difficulty with?"

"Well I'm not really having a difficulty with it but I'm amazed that you shave." He smiled at her as he spoke; it was actually a real turn on for him.

"So do you apparently." She noted using her coffee cup to point towards her son's junk.

"Yeah, that's a left over from when I dated Jenny Roth."

"Well mine is more because I like the way it feels, especially when I get wet and have a nice hard cock sliding in and out of me." She watched his reaction as she spoke so wantonly. She could see his erection beginning to form under the sheet; boys are so easy she thought. "There is something about the feel of skin on skin. Especially, drenched, slick skin, that's become hard sliding on a sodden, sopping, sloppy wet, pussy needing to be fucked and sucked. Now that's a turn on don't you think?"

Again she watched her son shift in the bed as his erection began to make itself known, his face reddening and his body shifting nervously in the bed. She would definitely be fucking him again today and if she was lucky, tomorrow and the day after.

"So when did you lose your virginity?" Rachel inquired, not sure she really wanted to hear the answer. But she felt sorry for his nervousness and wanted to keep the conversation going.

"Two years ago." He said straight out hoping that would be the end of it.

"And?" She let the questioning tone hang in the air.

"And it was Jenny Roth."

"Oh okay the one that liked you shaved, that makes sense. I remember her now; she was the one with the teeth." An odd pang of jealousy shot through her as soon as she heard the name. She felt very high school in her retort. Thinking to herself 'Oh my god what am I fifteen all over again, having a fit because my boyfriend dated other girls.'

"She had braces mom, they were the invisible ones. And it was just her front two teeth that were out of place."

"So braces and pubic hair, I get why she wanted you to shave." Rachel responded trying to get her jealousy in check. "Yeah well she was cute, even if her smile crooked. Did she shave too?"

"Yeah." His answer was short and sweet but somehow he knew his mother wasn't going to leave it like that.

"Was it a landing strip, just the edges or was she bald?"

"She was shaved bald."

"Did you like that?" She asked.

"Yes." Again his reply was brief.

"Do you like how I look?" She asked.

"Very much." He replied honestly.

"I like the way you look too." She blushed

"Thanks." He said.

"Would you like me bald?" She asked.

"If you want but I like the way you are now too." He was getting aroused and nervous all at the same time.

"So tell me more about this girl." Rachel saw her son's nervousness and taking pity on him decided to change the subject.

"What do you want to know?" He asked.

"What else did you like about her?" Again she could feel herself getting jealous anticipating the answer.

"I thought her smile was one of her best features." He replied.

"One of her best features, were there others, more sexual in their nature?"

"Well she did have a nice rack." He whispered under his breath as he looked down at his chest.

"I heard that. You always were a 'Boob Man' even when you were a baby. So was she your one and only?" She was smiling as she took in a deep breath asking the last question and shook her head allow her dark brown hair to cascade down her shoulders. She was doing her best to look enticing and provocative, after all she was thirty-eight and he was nineteen, girls his age had youth and perky tits on their side. Again with the jealousy, she really had to get that in check. She had no idea where this was coming from. Suddenly she was an insecure high school kid with a crush on some boy way out of her league. Or maybe she was in love with someone half her age and way out of her league. Either way her insecurity was causing her to feel threatened and this drove her need to secure her lover.

"No, she wasn't." Now he was feeling embarrassed, he wasn't too sure about sharing his sex life with others especially his mother. But given the recent change in their relationship he really didn't know how to respond so he settled for the truth.

"Oh really? I know this is a little late but you did use protection?" She hadn't even thought about Michael having an active sex life. Aside from the health risk associated with unprotected sex, her mind started to wander to other things, 'Oh god he's been with other girls, younger girls, beautiful hot girls with tight bodies... STOP IT!' She was going to make herself nuts.

"Yes mom. All the time." He reassured her.

"Well you didn't today." She was not only admonishing him but herself as well with that statement.

"Well things kind of got away from me here. You gotta admit this is a little crazy?" He replied not really knowing how to tell his mom that it was her lust that did him in, along with some crazy desire he really didn't know he had until recently. Cumming inside her was an extreme thrill he hadn't really thought of before. It wasn't just the feeling of skin on skin it was something more, something visceral that he couldn't place but the need to cum in her was strong and he wanted to do it again despite the risk. "It's not every day that my life goes wild like this."

"Well things get crazy for you and you forget to use a condom how does that happen? What if I'm pregnant?" It was only as she said it that the thought really began to sink in. Oddly she didn't seem as concerned as she thought she should, in fact she felt rather titillated and aroused by the idea of her own son knocking her up, it was an odd sensation and one she would have to revisit sometime. "What if you knocked me up?"

For his part Michael blushed at the thought. He really didn't know how to answer that question or whether it was a question as it seemed to be more of a statement. He did know that he tingled at the idea and it caused a surge of blood to stiffen his already hardened cock. He could feel the mushroom head of his prick flaring in what was most likely pride. To be prideful at what had just taken place between he and his mother seemed somehow diametrically opposite to what he should be feeling. He knew he should be feeling shame, embarrassment, shock, those types of emotions associated with breaking mores, and deeply entrenched values and yet he felt none of those things. He was highly aroused, excited, and gleeful even, and when his mother had said the word pregnant he felt exuberant and yes prideful, 'surely he was seriously fucked up' he thought.

"So mister did you think about that when your prick was buried deep in my vagina? Did you think as you filled my womb with your cum that you could be knocking me up, did you?" She asked with no actual hint of condemnation in her voice. Nothing to indicate that she even was concerned, her tone might as well have been more easily placed around a discussion of what would you like for supper than the seriousness of being made pregnant by ones son.

"No." Was his straight out answer.

She put her coffee cup down and brought both her hands to her hips. Slowly she slid them over the slight roundness of her tummy, her arms coming together causing her breast to push together further exaggerating their fullness. Her erect nipples stood out proudly as her hands moved down toward her sex. There was nothing she was doing that she wasn't conscious of, she knew the impact these movements were having on her son. She chose her words.

"Look at my pretty pink cunny, it's still slick with your cum." Her hands were now on either side of her sex pressing gently enough to only slight expose her inner labia.

Michael's only response was an almost audible gulp and to continue to stare at his mother's shaved pussy.

"Your seed is inside me baby. Your cock was so tight against my cervix some of your cum must've got into my womb." The index finger of her right hand began to gently pull her lips apart exposing her wet inner folds and the hard nub of her clitoris.

"I don't think you really thought this through when you decided to bang me with that big hard cock of yours, did you she asked her hands still gently exploring her sex.

"AAHhh n-no no not really." He was becoming more nervous than aroused now.

"Me neither, so if this happens again we're going to have to be more careful aren't we?" She said leaving every indication that this was in all likelihood going to happen again.

"Yes mom a lot more careful." He really wasn't sure that he wanted to be careful, in fact he was leaning more towards the 'Crying havoc and letting lose the dogs of war, damn the torpedoes, full speed ahead' kind of stuff that always got him in trouble when he was a kid.

"So how many times have you done the deed?" Seeing the need to change the mood she switched the direction of the conversation, her curiosity and her jealousy were getting the best of her.

"No one calls it the deed anymore." He said smiling at her as she came and sat on the bed.

"Well then how many times have you had sex?" She asked as she moved toward him, pulling back the covers and getting into bed with him. He spread his legs without thinking, as she slip in between them, as if they'd been lovers for years instead of hours. She was lying on her stomach, perched up by her elbows, her face inches away from his growing erection.

"I've had sex nine times, mom." His voice cracked as he spoke directly. He was trying to assert himself but her sensuality was something to contend with that he had never ever dealt with before.

"All with the same girl?" She asked looking into his eyes as her fingers began to trace down the length of his shaft.

"N-No, not all with the same girl." This time his voice didn't crack as he spoke but his arousal was evident.

"So you've had nine lovers then?" She began to wrap her hand around his growing appendage, gently stroking it and bringing it back to life.

"No m-m-mom I've only been with th-th-three girls... and one woman." Her continued stroking of his shaft was really making it difficult to concentrate.

"Really and who was that?" She smiled, licking her lips as she spoke and gently placing a kiss on the head of his cock.

"You."

"Have any of these other girls... lovers, ever give you head?" She smiled squeezing his cock in her right hand and gently touching his balls with her left.

"Two." He was looking straight into eyes as they spoke.

"Have any of them ever been able to take it all?" There was a sparkle in her and a smile on her face as she spoke.

"No."

"Well then I guess you're in for a treat." And with that she smiled gave him a quick wink and parting her lovely lips in the shape of a perfect 'O', bent her head over and took half his cock immediately into her mouth. Her tongue wrapped around the head and then snaked its way down the shaft coating it with a thin film of saliva. His immediate reaction was a distinctively loud moan and his head tilted back as the pleasure of his mother's mouth on his hard shaft overwhelmed him send shock waves of pleasure throughout his body.

With a loud sucking pop she withdrew her head from his lap and with a deep gasping inhale of air, spoke. "There is an art to giving good head." She said as she continued stroking his cock while she looked at it admiringly.

"First thing a girl needs to know is when taking on a nice big cock is to take it slow." She emphasizing the words 'Take it slow.' With that she returned her attention to his hard member and casually licked the head and shaft. Still holding his cock in her right hand she began to slowly stroke it from the base to the tip.

"By the way." She paused and looked him straight in the eye before continuing, "That's just as important for you boys to know when servicing girls. No one wants Roger Ramjet zooming around down there all Wyllie-Nellie when they're getting head."

Again she enveloped the head of his shaft in her mouth, licking and sucking the tip, her tongue poking his urethra and twirling around the crown. The effect of this was to cause Michael to bring his head forward and stare directly in his mother's eyes. The look he gave her was a lust filled desire that sent chills down her spine, she knew her lover was going to fuck her senseless after this and she couldn't wait. She placed several gentle kisses on the tip before she spoke again. "Second most important thing to know is eye contact. In my experience this seems a little more important for men than it is women."

This time she stared directly into his eyes as she took him in her mouth, the effect was amazing, watching his face as she swallowed his cock. Her eyes were beautiful and bold as they showed both her passion, for what she was doing and her own desire. Just knowing it was her son's cock in her throat, a cock that had been buried deep in her pussy and was going to be buried there once again made her shiver with lust. Having his cock in her mouth, sliding over her tongue and down her throat, made her feel powerful and vulnerable all at the same time. The power came from watching his facial features as she took him, his eyes rolling into the back of his head, his mouth open as if trying to say something but having the words stuck in his throat, the way his body twitched and jumped with every move of her tongue or gentle scrape of her teeth against the head and shaft of his cock. The vulnerability came from the feeling generated by his powerful cock. It was longer and thicker than anything she had ever experienced before. This was a large cock.

In and out of her mouth she slid his length, almost to the point of gagging. Several times she held him at the back of her throat, creating a powerful vacuum effect with her mouth and throat, around the head of his enormous penis. All the while looking directly into his eyes, even as hers became teary, causing her mascara to streak down her cheeks. While she was upstairs she had gone deliberately into her bathroom and applied it knowing full well she was going to suck his cock like this and that the mascara would run. The effect it produced was devastating. She looked part nasty wanton slut and part vulnerable, defenceless women force to accommodate the large throbbing cock of her lover which she dutifully did, added to her allure this had almost made Michael ejaculate then and there.

Pulling her mouth off his cock, she swallowed deeply, the saliva and precum that had accumulated in her mouth. She cleared her throat and spoke. "The next most important thing to keep in mind is to pay attention to all the parts." She began stroking his cock with both her hands now.

"The cock is more than just the shaft, it's the head." She stated emphatically as she began looking over his shaft with a more critical eye. "God you're big baby."

"The ridge just under the head is a good place to start." She pointed out as she pulled down on his cock, hard with both hands causing the whole thing to stand up straight and proud accentuating the large bulbous head as the skin of the shaft was pulled tight. The whole thing glistened with a shiny sheen of spit. His testicles were tight and bulging as she squeezed the base in an effort to ensure he didn't cum too soon, she had plans for this cock and they included satisfying her own physical needs as well. Her tongue traced the ridge of his crown completely sending shivers of ecstasy throughout his groin. If she hadn't squeezed the shaft as she did he surely would have erupted in her hand.

"This beautiful little whole at the tip is called the urethra. Watch what happens when I do this." She took her tongue and brought it to the tiny slit poking into it with the tip of her tongue. She began to wiggle her tongue back and forth, driving the tip into the hole. Immediately Michael's shaft flexed and his testicles contracted as shivers of delight travelled down his shaft. His hands immediately jerked forward and were on her head. She smiled as he gently held her face and then let go relaxing his body.

"Of course there's the shaft." She said, moving her tongue away from the tip and tracing down the entire length, leave a wonderful trail of saliva in its wake.

"The base." She spoke again just before her tongue travelled around the bottom of the shaft. His cock head felt magnificent as it gently rubbed against her forehead. She began to place her lips at the base and sucked, giving him firm kisses that were accentuated with audible sucking pops.

"Oh we can't forget the balls." She gently took each shaved testicles into her warm wet mouth. She held them there letting the heat from her mouth permeate each testicle. His body at first tighten in reactionary reflex, but then relaxed, that's when she began to gently suck.

"Ohhhh, god!" He moaned aloud as his back arched. His testicles gently falling from her mouth as his body shuddered in pleasure. He wasn't sure how much more of this he could take.

"Under the balls." No sooner had she said this, then her tongue began to swirl under his scrotum and move slowly south. There was a devious smile on her face as she licked the sensitive skin under his balls. The smile continued as she spoke. "This is called the perineum."

She began to delicately drawing little circles under his testicles with the tip of her tongue, up to and then over each one. At the same time she gripped his shaft tightly just under the head his cock with her right hand, her thumb began to lightly trace over the tip using the copious amounts of precum that gathered there as a lubricant. The slight tickling sensation of her tongue coupled with the movement of her thumb was bringing him to the edge very quickly.

"W-W-Where did you learn all th-th-this?" He asked as his body shivered with delight.

"Well in my day baby if you didn't want to lose your virginity you had to offer the boys something. This is what I had to offer, you like?"

"D-D-Definitely!" He sighed, knowing full well his mother must have been one hell of a Header Queen in her day. Surprisingly at this very moment that thought didn't really disturb him.

Rachel's continued to lick and suck his shaft and balls as she stroked his cock. Then taking pause she leaned forward.

"Oh and if the boy is really important to you and you really want to show him a good time, there's the anus." Again the smile returned to her face as she drove her tongue to the very spot she spoke of, driving her tongue deeply into his anus.

"Arrrgghhgh." Michael groaned and his knees flexed up, his mother's grip on his cock tightened as she squeeze the base. Her tongue pushed into his anus past the muscle of his sphincter. The thick warm muscle of her tongue invading his body, push deep and opening him up to the attack of tongue. No one had ever done that to him in all his life the effect was amazing. As she gripped his shaft tightly at the base she could feel the pulse of his prostate as it attempted to force his ejaculate from his balls up the shaft of his cock and out. Her grip remained tight and forced his cum to subside although the throbbing agony was almost as intensely pleasurable as it would have been had he spewed his cum all over his chest. Once his spasms subsided she spoke again.

"It is also important that you smile every once in a while. Look your lover in his eyes; let them know you like it, that you're having a good time too." Her own broad smile reinforced her love and passion for what they were doing.

"Use your hands and mouth at the same time. This not only increases his pleasure and changes up the sensations but it gives your jaw a rest. Not all boys cum quickly, some build up to it will others just pop." His eyes rolled into the back of his head as she spoke, he thought at that moment he would likely die of extreme pleasure if it was at all possible. Cumming and going at the same time.

"Oh the other most very important thing is saliva. Lubrication always makes things go well. Remember, the slicker the better." She immediately began to drool large amounts of saliva all over his cock causing the shaft to glisten. Her hand continued to slide up and down his length making him slick and wet. She then sat up on her knees, holding his cock in her right hand while her left gently grabbed and massaged his balls. She stroked him over and over feeling the tension in his body build again towards his climax.

"Now you're girl, you're bitch, you're slut, whatever." Rachel said dismissively, still having trouble with her jealous nature. "She also needs to know one thing for certain, how to breathe. Choking and gagging may look fun and wild in porn but in real life it's usually a deal breaker."

"When I've decided it's time to try the whole thing I find it's best to take a deep breath just before I go. That way I can take a relaxing breath out when I've reached my maximum depth." She said grinning like the cat that ate the canary. She knew the term maximum depth made her son's eyes light up. It was at that point that her head dove straight down and she engulfed his cock, taking it almost to the base. His body tensed and arched up as he grabbed the sheets, fighting the urge to grab his mothers head and push it the rest of the way down his shaft. He had heard her reference to gagging but at this point he didn't much care, his selfish male ego wanted head and the urge to hold her head in place was quite strong.

Just before he reached the point of no return his mother came upright again releasing his cock from her throat. A mixture of her saliva and his precum glisten all over her face as her dark mascara ran down the sides of her cheeks. She allowed their combined juice to flow out over her bottom lip down her chin and to slowly spill over her succulent breasts. 'God she looked fantastic.' Michael thought to himself.

"The next to last thing to remember now is rhythm. It's important to develop a good rhythm. All these things need to come together in producing the ultimate blow job." And with that said down she went again just as far as the last time holding herself there for mere seconds and then coming back up for air. She held herself again for a moment catching her breath, both hands stroking his cock and then back down she went. She repeated this practice a total of six more times, each time taking more and more of his cock until the last occasion when she took his entire cock to the base. Her nose was pushed up hard against his groin as she held herself there longer than she had previously done. He could feel the back of her throat give and allow him access. Her tongue pressed hard against his shaft pulsing as she held herself in place, the feeling was extraordinary. Then suddenly with a loud gasp she was up and only slightly chocking. Again her eyes watered and her mascara ran, saliva and precum covered her chin as it cascaded down her neck to her breast. In any other circumstance her appearance would be appalling but just now, to Michael it was the most erotic thing he had ever witnessed. Once she was able to catch her breath she spoke.

"I know I know I said no choking but I couldn't help it you have one fucking big cock." She smiled broadly as she wiped her chin. She was at that moment prideful on two separate levels. One was in her achievement at deep-throating her son's cock and the other was in her son's magnificent cock. After all she had a hand in creating it.

"And finally," She spoke again taking more time to regulate her breathing, "there's partner participation." She looked directly at Michael. "Not really important for the girl but the boys seem to like it, let's them feel as if they're in charge of the whole thing."

With that said she reached forward and took Michael's hands in hers and brought them to her body. Now she was leaning over him and her breasts were easier to reach and hold. She placed both of his hands on each of her breasts and squeezed. Then leaving his hands there on her breast to continue squeezing her flesh, she brought her own to each side of Michael's head and kissed him more passionately than she had ever kissed anyone before. The eroticism of this kiss was apparent to both of them and to any observer the lust ridden exchange of lips, tongues and saliva would have either caused great personal arousal or embarrassment.

Michael could taste his precum on his mother's lips and wasn't immediately sure how to respond but the invasion of her tongue and the suction of her mouth and lips didn't give him much opportunity to protest, however futilely. It was in this kiss between two people who should never kiss like this that Michael and his mother fell in love. It was this kiss that doomed both of them to this path from which neither would ever want to leave. Whatever happened next they both wanted it and needed it, they could not be apart and were bonded not only as mother and son but as lovers. Rachel felt her heart move towards her son in a way she had never thought it could. He was becoming her lover and she his, there would be no denying how they felt towards each other. The difficulty now was going to be the rest of the world and more crucially how they were going to deal with her husband.

Quickly the worries of tomorrow faded as the lust of today took its place. Both mother and son were again lost in the sexual fervour that had become their life at this moment. Each wanted nothing more than the pleasure of the other and Rachel wanted her son to experience everything she had to offer.

"Now a good finesse player will add a few extras to her game, such as vocals." Rachel said as she pulled herself away from the kiss. Breaking away from Michael at that point was very difficult, she knew if she didn't she would just end up fucking him and this whole exercise was about the ultimate blow job, she'd fuck him later. She'd fuck him a lot later, over and over again.

Again sitting upright on her knees between her son's legs she composed herself for the task at hand. She began to stroke his beautiful cock and smiled at him wickedly. Then moving closer, bringing her face to his balls all the while smiling that wicked smile, she slowly sucked his left testicle into her mouth, held it there gently and released it only to then suck the other testicle into her mouth. After she released his other testicle she licked his shaft all the way to the tip, never breaking eye contact. She placed a soft kiss on the tip of his penis and then spoke.

"Ummm. Ohhh god baby you have such a big cock." Her stroking became more deliberate and her pace quickened. She again brought her mouth to the head of his cock and took his shaft into her mouth half way covering it with her saliva.

"I love how your dick tastes in my mouth." She said again sucking his cock a little deeper into her mouth combining all the skills she had outlined earlier, setting the pace, keeping eye contact, lots of lubrication and a perfect use of hands and mouth together. "Fuuck I can hardly wait till you cum. I'm going to swallow everything you have to give me."

Michael was going to go over the edge now he was too far gone to hold off. It had taken everything he had not to cum. In fact if it wasn't for his mom squeezing technique he would have blown his load a while ago.

"I'm going to make you fucking blow." And with that said Rachel dove onto his engorged cock and took him completely to the base. She reached over and grabbed Michael's right hand placing it on her head and pushed down indicating what she wanted him to do. Her head bobbed up and down on his shaft and Michael held her as she had shown. She then grabbed his other hand and brought to her head as well pushing down hard indicating to Michael to be more forceful, to which he did. The subsequent groan that escaped her mouth as he began to force her head up and down his shaft incited Michael further and he began to fuck himself in and out of his mother's mouth.

"Oh fuck. Oh you fucking slut, you cock sucking fuck slut you're going to make me cum you bitch!" Michael's shaft continued to slide in and out of his mother's mouth as her delight in the pleasure she was affording him became evident. In and out he went until he could take no more. And when she knew he was close, as close as he had ever been his mother had one more trick. She took her index finger brought it to his anus and pushed.

"FUUUuuuckkk!" He roared as his ejaculate coursed through his cock. His mother's finger had penetrated him where nothing before today ever had. She could feel his prostate spasm and she gently massaged it as his buttocks tightened and his orgasm soared. One two three large volleys of cum exited the head of his shaft blanketing her throat. On the third one she pulled up and brought his cock into her mouth so that she could taste him. For her this act solidified her love for him and now she would give him anything, her body was his to explore, her heart was his to love, and her soul was his to keep. For Michael he knew he could never give this up, his relationship with his mother had changed and he didn't care who knew it, if he could he stay this way forever because that's the way lovers think.

Chapter 7
The Talk

Rachel was in the kitchen putting dishes away when Michael walked in. They had both showered and dressed, if you could call it that. Rachel was wearing one of Michael's sports jerseys and a pair of white cotton panties and Michael had on a T-shirt and a pair of boxers. For a summer day it was quite mild, with the promise of warming up later on that afternoon, so neither of them felt a need to wear more than was necessary. They had showered separately; Rachel felt that it would be the only way that either of them would get out of the shower with any hot water left. Showering together maybe romantic and very sensual but it didn't really lend itself to the practicalities of getting clean. So once dressed they each began to move through their morning routines like any other day.

Upon walking into the kitchen he immediately saw that his mom had set the table and the spot where he normally sat had a place setting with a plate with a sandwich on it. As she busied herself putting away the silverware, Michael couldn't help but notice the smell of her shampoo and the scent of her clean fresh skin which filled the kitchen, it gave him a warm contented feeling deep inside that he hadn't really noticed before. Her smells were everywhere throughout the house, the kitchen, the living room, her bedroom, he knew which rooms she frequented simply by the smell. Her hair was still wet and hung in dark curls across her shoulders and down her back. Although she had dried herself before getting dressed the jersey, his jersey, clung to her in all the right places accentuating the shape of her breast, the curve of her waist and the flare of her thigh. The jersey was barely long enough to cover her panties which peek through just below the hem. There was something remarkably sexy about this look, provocative yet understated. Her long shapely legs stood out even more and the fact that she was bare foot drove Michael instantly crazy as he openly stared at her.

"Sit down and eat, you'll need your strength." The inference was blatant and deliberate and caused Michael to startle before he spoke.

"Thanks for lunch," he said as he sat down at the kitchen table. Rachel had prepared a nice roast beef sandwich with lettuce, tomato, onion, mustard and mayo on a Kaiser roll, with a slice of mozzarella cheese. He had always been the envy of the other kids at school when he came with lunches like these. On occasion he actually sold or traded his lunch to kids for things of considerable value, CD's, Play Station or Xbox games you name he'd gotten it for a simple bagged lunch. 'Fuck people are crazy' he thought.

"You're welcome baby," she replied as she continued putting away dishes. "There's more if you want it."

Michael nodded his thanks as he began to stuff his mouth full of the roast beef sandwich. Rachel continued cleaning up the kitchen, wiping down the counter top and putting the utensils in the dishwasher. She went to the cupboard and took out two glasses and walked over to the fridge. Opening the door she took out the milk and poured herself and her son a glass which she promptly placed on the table for him. A routine she had done over and over again throughout Michael's life, she loved taking care of him, sometimes to the point of doting over him. The only difference this time was how provocatively she was dressed or more to the point undressed. As she placed his glass on the table her breast firmly rubbed up against his back, her hair dangle on his shoulder lightly touching his face, her hand held his shoulder firmly yet with a gentle loving pressure, these gestures were definitely different than before in their meaning and intent. She returned to the counter, placed her glass down and turning around promptly hopped up on the counter facing Michael. She didn't bother to cross her legs as personal modesty seemed a little silly now. Her legs were open, knees bent, gorgeous calves dangling in front of her; she definitely was at her best. This pose served to reveal her panty-clad sex, accent the flare of her hips, her tampering waist and full breast again she was hot and she knew the effect it was producing, God she was gorgeous. It was at that point that Michael realized that the very nature of his relationship with his mom was in fact changing. Here she was doing all the same things she had historically done but in a vastly different way. Now she was dressed in his jersey, wearing only a pair of white cotton panties, she was touching him, caressing him so much so that if he didn't quit focusing on her, he was going to have another erection to deal with. This was a significantly different turn.

He was her son and yet he felt different toward her. Sure some of the same feelings were there, he loved her but somehow it was different. He had mixed emotions. At some point he began to feel possessive, of course her ecstatic cries of joy and her emphatic statements that she was his, didn't dissuade him from this kind of thinking. If anything it drove him to be more possessive. And yet he knew there were boundaries in place, limits, things he could and could not do. Finally there was his father. He could not forget his father, he actually liked his dad, loved his dad and yet he was now competing with him over the same women, god this was twisted. So much so there was a part of him that was determined not to lose the competition.

"Mom?" Michael's voice was tentative as he spoke. There was an edgy nervousness to his tone. He sounded almost apprehensive.

"Yes," Rachel answered sensing the underlying nervousness in her son's voice.

"Have things changed between us?" he asked, his emotion mixed as he spoke. Part of him didn't want to hear the answer to this question. Part of him wanted things to be as they were and yet his heart wanted more.

"How do you mean?" She said not giving him a direct answer, wanting to see where he was going with this line of questioning.

Things of course had changed and would forever be different between them but just exactly how only these next few moments would tell. Of course she was his mom and as such she took care of him without thought, it was truly selfless. She made his lunch, washed his clothes, sometimes putting them away and frequently she picked up after him so that his father wouldn't be driven mad by the mess he left about. She was his mom, he had never really regarded her differently, not that he deliberately took advantage of her attending to him but the expectation was there, unwritten but there. A social code different from other social codes, she didn't take care of his father in the same way. With his father there was more give and take and less servitude, less obligation to mother. There were times when she certainly held his father to a different standard. Sure she may have loved him but she didn't mother him, far from it. So here is where Michael began to worry and not strictly from a selfish place, he knew he should do more and in fact he would do more, but he didn't want to lose the mother/son relationship he cherished and so dearly loved and appreciated.

They were at a crossroads for sure but the paths they were looking to travel down were not as simple as just going left, right or straight ahead and there was certainly no going back. They had said and done things that made everything different now, she had done things, said things and although she knew they did not fit social norms, she was too deeply affected by them to simply change her mind and pretend they had never happened. That line of thinking was too juvenile, too pedestrian. So he pondered her question, how did he mean exactly?

"I don't know? Have they changed, are we so different now?" he paused not knowing where to go. "Well I know we're still mother and son but we certainly are doing a few non-mother and son things don't you think?"

"Yes we are," she replied. "Michael, are you ok with what's happened between us?"

Rachel turned to face Michael; she knew this conversation was bound to happen sooner or later she had just thought that it would be a little later than this. For her part she really hadn't put together much in the way of analysing where their relationship was headed. In her heart she knew Michael would go off to school, find a girl, get married, create a life of his own, but in her fantasy, her rapid fire adrenalized sex talk, she was everything from seductress to sex slave and in that there seemed to be no thought of him not being there. She was his, he was hers on whatever level he deemed fit.

The next statement out of his mouth took Michael an enormous amount of personal strength to say. He didn't want to ruin what he had just experienced, he rather enjoyed it but at the same time he didn't want to lose what they had. He just didn't know how they could live with the duality of their relationship and his young mind couldn't put into words the complex set of emotions associated with that thought.

"Yes mom I am but what has happened between us does make things different, I feel different about you."

"Ok, how so?"

"I don't know just different, kinda possessive I guess. I don't want to lose you, I'm not sure I want to share you. I'm not sure about a lot of things."

"Baby how do you eat an elephant?"

"Not funny mom." That had been one of his mother's favourite sayings all through his life. How do you eat an elephant? As stupid as it sounded the answer was relatively simple, one bite at a time. In other words slow down you're getting way ahead of yourself. Take your time don't go so fast. It was her answer for the impatience of youth.

"Wow babe you're getting way ahead of yourself here. Where are you?" The concern in her voice now mimicking the look on her face as she began to feel real distress for her son and his current predicament, one she was partially responsible for.

"I don't know mom confused I guess." The more Michael thought about their relationship, the more he tried to put some perspective on it and the more overwhelmed he became. He had no frame of reference for what they were currently experiencing, two days ago she was his mom, plain and simple and his only goal was to see if he could get her to let him stay out later than he should or not have her catch on to the fact that he hadn't made his bed or taken out the garbage. Crazy fantasies were one thing but reality is a whole other set of circumstances.

"Ok then, do you want to stop?" The words were out before she knew she had said them. They sounded abrupt to her and almost gave away the pain she felt as she said them. Again it was her nurturing nature coming forward, wanting to protect her son from harm putting his concern ahead of hers. She knew what they were doing was frowned upon, some might say wrong or immoral but she couldn't help how she felt.

Michael felt panic hit him fast and hard, his stomach tightened and he froze. He didn't even contemplate stopping or ending what was going on between them he just wasn't sure what it meant or how to deal with it. Were he and his dad going to duke it out on the front lawn over his mother, were they going to share her, was his mother going to leave his father. Better yet, how did his mother feel toward him or about his dad now? It was a lot to process but the answer to her question was an emphatic, "No!"

No god help him he didn't want to stop, if anything he wanted more. He wanted it all. He wanted his mom the women who took care of him selflessly without thought. He wanted the nurturer, the supporter, the caregiver. And more importantly he wanted the desperate, wanton women who rock his world and brought him more unadulterated pleasure than he had ever imagined was possible. He wanted the nasty, slutty women who knew how to fuck, take cock, and give back as good as she got if not better.

"Alright then, neither do I," she said as simple as that. "Come here."

It was less of a command and more of a request but still Michael wasn't going to disregard it. He got up from the table and approached his mother. She was still sitting across from him on the counter. Her legs spread wider as he approached and her arms were opening to receive him in a hug.

"Look baby things have changed between us. They are going to be different. You can't enter into a sexual relationship with someone and expect things not to change."

Wrapping her legs around him, she pulled him in close and draped her arms over his neck. She smiled as she spoke, "Do you love me?"

"Yes."

"Good cause I love you too," she said in return. Her eyes stared deep into his as they spoke. Her nose and mouth mere fractions away from his face and lips, he could feel her warm breath on his face, smell her sweet scent, and she was intoxicating. He was relieved to hear her words, immensely relieved. Of all the emotions running through him that one was the strongest was his sense of relief.

"Are there other girls in your life?" She looked him square in the eye as she spoke, "Be honest."

The question threw him at first but he answered it anyway, "Yes."

"Well there is another man in mine too." She said, "And we both know who he is."

"I know that."

"Well, he's not going away any time soon." She said matter-of-factly.

"I know that too," he said. "And to be honest I don't want him to."

"Good." She continued to hold him not breaking eye contact as she spoke, "Do you find me sexy?"

"Oh god mom you don't know how much."

"Good cause I definitely find you sexy too," and with that she pulled him closer. Her panty-clad sex began to rub against his ever present bulge. They could both feel the heat generated from where their bodies touched. Her eyes stared into his, they were wide and open and unbelievably beautiful. Their lips and mouths almost touching as they spoke.

"Mom?" he said his voice beginning to shake.

"Yes baby?" her voice becoming seductive and her tone soft and deep as she spoke. Her lips caressed his in all but a kiss. He wanted to taste her mouth with his, press his lips to hers, touch her tongue with his tongue in a kiss that would make time stop.

"I'm getting horny." Michael turned red as he spoke, "I don't mean to but you're just..."

"Well," Rachel paused briefly before she next spoke. "That's because we've become lovers."

Her mouth opened as it came into contact with his. Their lips softly touched and then their tongues. Quickly what started as a gentle kiss became more forceful and deliberate. Rachel pulled him into her with a fluidity and sensuality that singled only one thing, her need to fuck.

Michael's body became rigid, a foundation upon which she could move and undulate against. Her hips began to writhe against his causing his cock to harden further and become even more erect, if that was possible. The bulge in his underwear was massive, threatening to rip through his boxers. Her breasts heaved upon her chest as she mashed them into his torso, her hard nipples poking him signalling her arousal. With her left hand she held the back of his head while her right slid between them in an attempt to excavate his cock from its cloth prison.

Breaking there kiss in a heavy breath she spoke, "Come here baby, come let me see it."

She immediately grabbed a hold of his raging weapon and pulled it free from its constraints. As soon as her hand came in contact with the head she felt the copious amount of precum emphasizing his arousal. This coupled with her own anticipation caused her to become wet and wanting. Gripping the shaft firmly she began to stroke his rigid member, rubbing her thumb across the dark purple mushroom head smearing his precum causing Michael to groan loudly.

With both hands Michael pulled his boxer's down over his hips and let them fall to the ground, fully releasing his sex. His hands wrapped around her hips pulling her close. He was fully locked in another kiss and didn't want it to end. Not only did his body ache at this moment but so did his heart. He wanted this women fully and completely, body and soul. "Fuck I want you."

Having been drawn him closer Rachel began to stroke his cock much more deliberately. The head wet with precum skin stretched and taut looked menacingly bigger than ever. The young virulent cock threatening to rip her apart as it pressed into her, wanting entry into that most forbidden of places. It felt like steel in her hands covered in soft velvet, smooth and soft to the touch yet unbreakable and rock hard. Their lips locked together in a passionate kiss, tongues deeply exploring each other's mouths. It took everything she had to pull her mouth away from his. "Do you want to fuck those other girls?"

"Not right now."

"At least you're honest," she smiled as she spoke.

"I'm not supposed to lie to my mother."

"No baby, no you're not." Again another smile came across her face as she placed her forehead to his and breathed in deep. The air around them now seemed electrically charged. The both exuded a sexual tension that threaten ignite the room if it wasn't soon quenched.

"I'm not supposed to fuck my mother either."

"No baby you're not supposed to fuck your mother, but you're going to." She smiled a devious smile now as she spoke, "Oh by god you're going to."

They continued to kiss and suck each other's mouths like ravenous wolves devouring their prey. Wet deep kisses of passion, like lovers who had been lost to each other for years and were only recently found.

"Oh and baby one of those times when you decide you're going to fuck one of those other girls" She paused to look deep in his eyes as she spoke so he knew she meant what she was saying. "I get to watch."

His excitement and arousal soared at hearing her words. He wasn't sure he had heard them right and his face was a mask of bewilderment.

"That's right baby I get to watch," she said as she continued to stroke his engorged penis, smearing his precum over the head and down the shaft. "I get to watch you fuck them with this big hard cock and stretch their tiny little pussy like you do mine."

She smiled as she spoke in hushed terms, licking her lips, "And when you fill their wet dripping cunt with your cum I get to have that too."

She knew this kind of talk would bring him over the edge and make him want to ravish her. "Can you handle that baby, can you handle watching mommy eat and suck cum out some young tighty's pussy after you've filled it with your hot wet load?"

He pressed his cock into her panty clad pussy stretching the material pushing it into her wet centre. He was so hard he believed that he could actual push through the material ripping it as he entered her. He could feel her clit as it pressed against him signalling her own arousal. He pushed harder capturing her hand between his sex and causing her to let go of his cock. Immediately she brought it up to her mouth and began lick his fluids off her palm and from between her fingers.

The taste of his precum drove her wild and caused her pussy to flutter with anticipation. She was filled with so many desires at once. She wanted to fuck him, to stroke him, to suck him and to have him suck her. Fast, slow, long, short, hard or gentle she didn't care as long as she had him inside her somehow, mouth, tongue or fingers.

"You're going to make me cum!" she said in a forceful tone.

"Take my panties off! Take my panties off!" She had demanded more than asked and he complied. As her mouth pulled away from his to take in vital air he looked at her almost bewildered. They were both gasping and breathing deep. With both hands he reached for her panties and pulled them down over her hips. She placed both her hands on the counter, lifting herself up so that he had less trouble relieving her of the now cumbersome article of clothing. As flimsy as they were they impeded her desire and that was all that mattered, to have some part of him inside her now.

As he pulled her panties down he noticed that the gusset clung to her sex, which was thoroughly soaked from the flow of her arousal. He continued to pull them down across her thighs, over her knees to her ankles where she kicked them off and sent them flying across the room. Once free she repositioned herself on the counter bringing her right foot up to rest on the counters edge. She spread her legs apart with both hands giving him full access to her exposed sex. Her scent flooded the room and filled his senses, his arousal piqued beyond measure. Whether she pushed him or he dove, either way his head was buried between her legs faster than either of them thought possible. Immediately his mouth latched onto her sex, his tongue deeply exploring the orifice that caused them both extraordinary delights. He drank deeply from her centre lapping up her flow and adding his saliva to her already soaked cunt. Her hips moved and undulated with each probing movement of his tongue. His oral prowess amazed her and at that very moment she didn't know which she wanted more the huge thick piece of meat that hung menacingly between his legs or his insanely penetrating tongue.

"Fuck you bastard! God what you do to me." Rachel convulsed as she spoke her body reacting to what he was doing to her. Her body arching back, forcing her arms back behind her for support as her knees pulled up, her feet and ankles wrapping around Michael's head. Her breasts jutted outward on her chest, nipples hard as diamonds, her head and neck stretching back as her first orgasm took her.

Michael continued to lick her labia, her pussy opening to him like the most erotic flower. Copious amounts of fluid appeared to pour from her centre as he lavished her sex with soft succulent kisses. His tongue gently moved over the mouth of her sex down to her perineum and then ever so gently over the beautiful rosebud that leads to her darker passage.

Rachel's body tingled and vibrated as Michael sucked and licked her through her orgasm. Her mind was in a fog of ecstasy and wasn't quite registering where his ministration were exactly taking him. When his tongue did finally stop its progression she became vaguely aware of where he was stationed. The sudden but gentle warm piercing of his tongue into her anus brought about an unexpected second orgasm, much different from any she had ever experienced before.

"OOOHhh Gawdd!!" She groaned.

Sudden warmth radiated outward and down her thighs to her knees while at the same time travelling up and over her groin into her tummy and around her back. It was quickly followed by an almost intensely electric pleasure that crackled through her being again causing her to lunge forward wrapping her entire body around her lovers head and shoulders.

"Fuuuck!" Was the next word she spoke as her body convulsed again for second time. She held Michael tightly to her groin as the bliss and rapture of her orgasm took her. Her eyes rolled back into her head, her legs and thighs shaking and the warmth that travelled through her core began to become increasingly intense at her aperture of her sex.

The flood of liquid that gushed forth from her body both startled and amazed Michael when it happened. He had seen girls squirt on the internet before but had never experienced it. Unlike some he was not repulsed by his mother's carnal display of erotic rhapsody and joy but rather he revelled in it.

Michael became vaguely aware of the sobs that emanated from his mother's core. Her hands were at either side of his head as she gently pulled him away from her sex tilting his head up to look him in the eyes.

"I love you, I love you, I love you." Tears were in her eyes as she softly spoke. Gently she pulled him up to her mouth so that she could kiss him. Her deep gratification apparent as she licked and sucked his face of the copious fluids deposited there. Michael was unsure of what to do next, her actions appeared markedly different from her expression which looked both distraught and erotic at the same time, if that were possible.

"Are you ok?" he asked feebly.

"Oh god yes," she replied. "More than you know."

"Do you want me to stop?"

"No, no never." She held his head as she spoke and continued to cover his face with gentle kisses. "In fact not to sound too greedy but I want more."

"What?" He smiled as he spoke.

"God I love you. Now eat mee!!" She laughed and gently pushed his head down to where he came from.

Soon Michael had her writhing again as brought her to the edge of yet another orgasm. Good lord she was greedy for them. Just as she felt the tell-tale signs of her next orgasm the phone rang. With Pavlovian like reflexes she had the phone in her hands before she realized what she had done.

"Hello," her voice was deep and gasping for breath as she answered. Michael's tongue continued to spear the depths of her sex. The warm wet malleable muscle that is his tongue, thick and probing moved past her vaginal lips into the centre of her being. Delving deep it brings with it the delicious ecstasy of being penetrated sexually by your lover. She cannot help but gasp as she speaks into the phone.

"Yes dear I'm ok." Immediately Michael knew it was his father. Her tone change and she attempted to concentrate as she spoke. Like some mad man he redoubled his efforts to increase his mother's arousal. She was his right now how dare this intruder interrupt their pleasure. He moved up and over the mouth of her sex, his wet lips sliding gently over the hood of her clitoris. He could feel the ever hardening bud beginning grow and become pronounced. He half expected his mother to push him away as she spoke on the phone but instead she gently held his head in place not wanting him to leave her.

"What am I doing?" Rachel paused for a minute as a mischievous thought crossed her mind. Her arousal got the better of her and in an instant she decided to go with it, pressing the boundaries and limits of propriety.

"Well do you really want to know?" Again the pause in her voice gave evidence to the playfully naughty side of her personality. So long had she hidden and buried it behind the façade of the proper wife and mother she had always portrayed.

"I'm sitting on the kitchen counter in one of Michael's old sports jerseys and a pair of cotton panties." Suddenly Michael panicked at the mention of his name. His heart quicken, if that was at all possible as it had been pounding in his chest ever since he began devouring his mother. He could feel the adrenaline coursing through is body causing his muscles to tingle. His immediate reaction was to pull away but his mother's reaction was quite the opposite. She quickly placed the phone in the crook of her neck and with both hands pushed his head forward forcing his mouth to her sex. Her hands remained there gently holding his head, fingering his hair as she ground her cunt into his mouth.

"Actually my cotton panties are on the floor." At that point Michael wished he could hear the other side of the conversation. Rachel's breathing became more exaggerated as the pleasure she was feeling intensified.

"Well no I'm not worried about him catching me," she said flatly as she looked down at Michael caressing his head and holding him firmly in place. His tongue began to dance over her clit in a very fast figure eight pattern that drove her further to the edge.

"I think you might be more concerned with the fact that my lover has his head between my legs and is making me very wet and horny." Rachel knew that this autoerotic conversation needed arouse all three partners, herself included. She could hear her husband's voice crack with excitement as he began stutter as he spoke. Michael needed to be assured she had no plans to change the direction they were headed and she needed to play with her nasty side.

"What no I'm trying to pay attention but he just took my clit into his mouth. And baby you know how sensitive I get after I cum." Her description was more than accurate Michael had taken her clit into his mouth and was gently sucking the well lubricated little man in the row boat. His tongue danced across her clit ever so gently in a back and forth motion that became a blur of movement. This exquisite activity shot vibrating jolts of pleasure out Rachel's legs causing her toes to curl. A flood of her vaginal juice began to pour copiously from the mouth of her sex as Michael appeared to take it all as though he was dying of thirst.

"How many?" Michael could almost hear the smile in her voice as she spoke. "Two maybe three-ee-e."

Again there was silence as Rachel attempt to listened to her husband, however maybe not as intently as he would've liked.

"Oh fuck yes," she moaned into the phone as her lover's mouth began to bring her closer to release. "What, no he just inserted two fingers into me."

Michael had done just that. His tongue remained tightly fixed to her clit as the index and forefinger of his right hand probed the open mouth of her sex. If she wasn't wet before, she certainly was now. His hand became soaked with her essence and her scent filled his nostrils arousing him further, pushing back whatever inhibition he had left.

"Oh gaaawwwddd! Oooohh fuuuck!" Again her lovers tongue pressed on her ever hardening clit as his fingers began to saw in and out of her body. "What baby, no I'm listening to you, yes he's going to make me cum."

Rachel's hips began to move and thrust forward on their own volition. Her legs shot forward and then squeezed together firmly holding Michael between her thighs. She could feel her orgasm radiating from her centre as the mix of emotions that accompanied it flooded her. Tears of joy blurred her vision as looked down at the young man that caused her heart to soar. It took her a minute to recover and hear exactly what the caller on the other end of the phone was saying.

"You wish you were here so you could watch," Rachel smiled at the thought of that. "Oh I don't know about that baby, do you think you could handle it? What if he wanted to fuck me?"

With that said Michael became wild in his efforts. Rachel had to bring her hand up to take the phone for fear she would drop it. She repositioned the phone to her other ear and with her right hand held Michael in place in an attempt to steady her impassioned lover. His magnificent tongue continuing to probe and lick her relentlessly, young and impatient his exuberance sometimes got away from him. Gently she moved his head from her centre in order to give her sensitive clit time to recover. "Easy there lover," she whispered.

She continued to hold his head for balance as his ministrations caused her to periodically lose her precarious perch on the counter. Sure it looked sexy sitting on the countertop legs spread wide, pussy dripping with your lover's head buried deep within your sex, but it didn't really lend itself to frantic passionate sexual congress. Hell if she wasn't careful she'd end falling breaking her arm and Michael's neck; now there's a story for the Paramedics.

"Does he want to fuck me? I don't know want me to ask him?" She looked down between her legs and saw Michael's head nodding quickly in affirmation. His mouth and tongue continued lick and suck but now more tenderly, more gently.

"He's nodding his head," she smiled as she spoke. "Where are you?"

"Oh, well then shut the door and lock it." Michael continued to lick and suck his mother's delicious twat. His father must be at work calling from his office. Michael knew his office was fairly large and rather private. He was after all on the twentieth floor, with no other large buildings around to have to worry about prying eyes.

"Are you comfortable baby? Again she paused before speaking waiting for an answer. "Ok, get your cock out for me and listen close while mommy gets fucked."

"Good boy." Michael was intensely curious as to what was being said on the other end on the line. He would have liked to hear both his parents talking but could guess by what his mother was saying just how the flow of the conversation went. "Are you stroking it? Good."

"Is he hard?" She paused a minute and giggled before she spoke, "What do you think baby he's eating my pussy how could he not be."

Rachel knew her husband's weaknesses and began playing to them. He wanted her to be forceful with him almost domineering but not quite. He wanted her to be gregarious and slutty to the point of being wantonly nasty and right now she wanted that as well. He wanted her to have a virile lover and get fucked by a really big cock and she also wanted that. He wanted to be there to watch and she was determined to provide him with the next best thing. A detailed description of her defilement as it was happening, not quite like being there but damn close.

"Yes he's big." She knew where this was going, he was so predictable. She didn't fancy herself to be a Size Queen she just like the fit of a cock inside her wet pussy. Size was never as important as skill.

"Bigger? Yes baby he's bigger... and yes thicker too." God he was much bigger and much thicker. Looking at his cock now she wondered how she had ever managed to fit it inside her.

"How much?" She knew he would ask, it always came down to size for him. "Oh baby do you really want to know?"

Of course he did he couldn't help it. Part of the fantasy for him was the thought of his wife receiving imaginable pleasure. Imaginable pleasures and countless orgasms, being completely taken and retaken, her pussy stretched and filled so that every nerve ending in her body tingled and hummed with sexual delight. If he could somehow retain the illusion that he commanded it, so much the better.

"Baby he's about twice as big and twice as thick." Michael hadn't known about his father's proportions and up to this point the thought had only been peripheral at best, however with his mother's statement he felt an extraordinary boost to his ego. 'The male ego was so fragile,' she thought. 'Boys should never share the shower in gym class.'

"Yes baby he's been in me before," her voice was teasing now deliberately. Michael was now standing up in front of her, his erection pointing up and away from his body at a forty-five degree angle, god it was magnificent.

"Do I want him in me again? Yes baby I do." She was being completely honest, she wanted him inside her again and again and again, it had been the most erotic experience of her life and she needed to feel that again. God did she ever, she was very horny now and describing what was happening, playing this deliciously devious game over the phone was making her even more horny, if that were at all possible.

"Baby you need to know something before we go there," she stroked Michael's cock back and forth as spoke into the phone while staring straight into his eyes.

"We don't have any condoms right now and I'm not on any protection yet." This had always been at the heart of the fantasy for her husband, bareback sex. Always the edge, always the risk, cross the line for the sake of pleasure and forget the consequences. Damn the torpedoes full steam ahead. She knew his answer before she spoke.

"Baby, are you sure? She paused, the last word of that sentence lingering in the air 'sure'. The silence between her next spoken words was deafening.

"What if he cums in me?" She had to put it out there, had to let him know. There could be consequences, repercussions some sort of aftermath.

"Oh honey I don't think he will and I'm not sure I want him to."

He had asked if he'd pull out Michael thought and his mother had said no. They were talking about him cumming inside his mother, not pulling out. This was a much deeper conversation and it was setting the ground work for where they were headed. He was going to be her lover, her real honest no holds barred lover and his father was going to consent to it all in that moment.

Chapter 8

At Night Everything Changes
(4 a.m.)

The moon shone through the window illuminating the room in a soft but hauntingly incandescent light. Darkness muted the colours of everything in the room giving them an almost smoky black and white glow. Images not quite black or white appeared to be basked in a supple smooth grey. All sharp edges and contrasts blended together making everything in the room appear less distinct. The only thing that stood out in the room was in the centre of the bed, two coupled bodies locked in a grippingly passionate embrace, oblivious to the world and its contrivances. Gone was the intense energy of electrified lust, the urgency of conquest, the immediacy of release which at one time drove the two to meet and couple where others knew better. In its place was passion, desire and above all else love.

All around the room were traces of force and movement, nothing placed carefully anywhere, clothing strewn across the floor where it had been thrown, ripped, pulled and torn from bodies intent on one goal; copulation. At one time the need for sex had dominated the atmosphere of this room. Release and surrender had been the protocol, greed and need the only driving goals but now the feel of the room had changed. The two bodies entwined in the centre of the bed, tightly embraced in a sensual, luxurious, sexy knot of arms, legs and skin sought neither release nor separation. Thrusts and jabs were replaced with sliding circular motions as sensual as dance, soft jazz or slow dirty blues. Sex was no longer the order of the day; it had been replaced with passion, desire and love.

"What am I going to do with you?" Rachel spoke softly to her lover as she gently kissed his forehead, nose and then mouth. "You have spoiled me for all others."

Her hair was matted to her forehead, her body glisten in sweat, and her skin tanned and supple glowed from the refreshing workout of sexual release. Her lover continued to slide his body along hers. His hard throbbing sex moving in and out of hers, causing sensual pleasures to course through both their bodies. The hard piercing sabre sliced slickly into her centre delving deeper than she had ever experienced before pushing its thankfully blunt end firmly against her cervix as he bottomed out inside her. She was gloriously filled and stretched to capacity, comfortably full and complete. The sights, sounds and smells of sex filled the room.

"There are others?" her lover replied softly as he gazed deeply into her eyes. They kissed again as his hips continued their in and out motion. Her legs spread opened wide to receive him allowing the flare of her hips to accept him further. Her legs wrapped around him holding him inside her body refusing to let him go. Each penetration bringing with it the glorious sensations of sexual pleasure and the anticipation of release.

"There are no others," she assured him quietly as she held him tighter to her pressing her body as close to his as she could get. It was a lie and they both knew it but neither wished to discuss it now, there would be time enough for that later. "There are no others."

Again the two lovers continued their sensual dance. Rachel spread herself wide to accommodate her lover, she was his now and she needed him to know it, if not by words than by actions. Her body opened and gave way to his, allowing him to take her again and again with every recurring plunge. Her mouth sought out his and their kiss ignited a passion that neither had known existed between the two. Deep in her heart Rachel was scared of the emotions she was feeling, the desire she was having towards her young lover. Her heart was his and she knew it but he was young and prone to foolishness as all young people are, he would not know what he held, what sacred trust had been passed on to him. Lovers of his age were inexperienced and self-centred. Sure in all likelihood he loved her, he even adored her but he would not be as deeply and passionately bonded to her as she was becoming to him. Her love in this short time was becoming obsessive and she knew it, which meant nothing but disaster for both of them. If she was not careful she would throw caution to the wind and risk everything for their passion. At this very moment he was buried deep inside her without benefit of protection. This would be the fifth, no sixth time she took him inside her within a twenty-four hour period without protection. Each time they had made love, fucked, rutted or tore into each other with abandon he had spent himself completely inside her. His ejaculate was always large and deep, leaving copious amounts of his seed deeply planted inside her unprotected womb. In every instance she had had an orgasm either before, during or after his release, causing her cervix to spasm and press down against her uterine wall in an attempt to capture and hold onto the valuable fluid deposited deep inside her body. Her body was becoming alive with the lust of wanting to be impregnated. The need for pregnancy had become a driving biological force pushing aside all reason. A baby lust was upon her if it could be called that and she would see it through if she was not careful. Her rational mind had nothing to say on the matter it was strictly biologic and her body craved the outcome of this copulation. Her womb wished to mate, to take her lover's seed deep inside her and create life. It did not care about age or other outside influences, all it wished for was that her hips spread wide and open, that the mouth of her sex stay wet and lubricated in order to receive the phallus it craved and that the seed that would impregnate her body regardless be planted deeply at the mouth of her cervix.

Their foreheads were pressed firmly against each other as they continued to fuck. Each breath coming from her was deep and steady, the intake of oxygen mixed with simultaneous gasp of pleasure as the thick truncheon he possessed moved in and out of her body. Their eyes were locked on each other, their bodies covered in a sheen of sweat, causing her breasts to look more pronounced as they sat high on her chest, nipples rock hard pointing straight out indicating her arousal.

"That's it baby fuck me," she moaned as he drove into her steadily. "Don't stop, just fuck me."

His body responded to her voice, the pace of his hips quickening as he bottomed out inside her with each beautifully aching thrust. He could feel her cunt continually grasping his cock. Her vaginal walls felt like velvet along the length of his shaft as he moved fluidly in and out of her. The bulbous head of his rigid cock repeatedly buffeted against her cervix, as he continue his delicious onslaught. In and out of her he slid, causing her womb to ache for his release.

"Oh god you drive me crazy I could fuck you all night," he stared directly at her, his eyes locked on hers as he spoke.

"You have," she replied kissing him passionately, her tongue invading his mouth, fervently duelling with his. This served to elicited greater zeal from her young lover as she encircled his neck with her arms drawing him closer. God she was beautiful, her sharp jaw and nose highlighted her beauty. Her eyes, half lidded, sexily peering into his, her mouth soft and sensual everything about her aroused him.

"Oh god, oh god I don't want to cum. I just want to keep fucking you." His body had found the perfect rhythm which she matched stroke for stroke. Together they moved on the bed as one singular organic being, shifting positions like practiced dancers. Missionary, scissor, doggy, cowgirl, butterfly, each position moving and sliding into the next, each penetration deeper and more excruciatingly delicious than the last he had no idea how long they had been making love but if the sun had come up at that moment he would not have been surprised.

"You're making me cum baby, you're making me cum," her body convulsed as she spoke.

He could feel every detail of her sex pressing against him as she rode him through her orgasm. Her clit pressed hard into his pubic bone. His cock continued to slice in and out of her as she shuddered beneath him. Suddenly her body convulsed her back arched up; both her hands took hold of his tight round buttocks and held him deep as she came. The continual spasm of her hips increased their mutual pleasure locking them deeply in this moment of rapture.

"Fuuucckkk!" was all she could say, the word got stuck in her throat. She spread herself wide to receive him, his cock buried deep inside her began to flex, and she knew he would cum and release his seed even though he fought it.

"Cum. Cum in me baby," it was a cross between a request and a demand. "Honey cum in me its ok, I want this more than anything, as much as I want you."

In and back, in and back, in and back, three half thrust were all he could manage as she held him so tight. The slurping wet sound of her sex was like nothing he had ever heard before, it was carnal. The suck and pulling sensation went right to his balls as though she were attempting to draw out his seed. He reached down with both hands and firmly grabbed each breast and squeezed. Bringing his thumb and forefinger together he pinched both nipples hard and twisted cause her to groan deeply and release her hold of him. In that moment he reasserted himself as the dominant and she accepted the fucking she was going to get now. She wanted his seed; she was going to get it.

Chapter 9
A Morning Full of Surprises
(24 hours later...)

"That's it suck my cock."

Michael could feel the head of his cock push into her throat. He knew she could supress her gag reflex and take him to the root; every time she did he became more and more impressed. Although his experience was somewhat limited he knew it would never get any better than this.

"Oh god that's it, all the way baby, all the way."

With each plunge her mouth made down his shaft he fought the urge to cum, knowing that the longer he delayed the greater the end benefit would be, still it was a difficult challenge.

"Fuck that's good."

Each rise and fall, each slow descent; each soft caress was punctuated with inaudible sounds and he more felt then heard. Soon this began to change as she sensed his arousal peeking. Her pace quickened, and the soft slow descents became more deliberate, more urgent, punctuated now with loud slurping sounds the result of the copious amounts saliva mixed with precum that now covered his shaft and balls.

"You have got to be the greatest cocksucker going. Fuck your good."

The dirty talk and praised seemed to excite her more and she noticeably doubled her efforts after each point of praise. Like Pavlov's dog salivating at the ringing of a bell, she salivated and gorged herself on his magnificent cock after each word. Now he had his hand on her head, fingers entwined in her hair, tentatively tightening his grasp and taking a more commanding role in this sexual encounter.

"Fuck you bitch; you're going to make me cum."

Again her head bobbed up and down his shaft, her pace frenzied and wild. Her actions seemed to suggest that she couldn't seem to get enough of him. Up and down her mouth travelled as she took him deep into her throat, pass her gag reflex, pressing her lips and nose tightly against his pubic bone.

"What has gotten into you, wholly fuck!"

No sooner did he ask then she pulled her mouth of his raging hard on and spoke. A loud gasp of air accented just how forceful she had been at sucking his cock. Her face wet and covered with the slim of their engagement, she licked her lips and spoke, eyes glazed and staring at him. "I can taste her on your cock!"

It had done something to her, made her insatiable and wanton. She felt slutty and dirty and nasty all at the same time. She knew she should be repulsed by it but instead she was aroused, thrilled, her mind running wild with the images of Michael having sex with the young blonde bimbo that had come to her door earlier that morning, looking for her son, her lover, her man.

(18 hours before...)

When the doorbell rang Rachel was in her housecoat. She wasn't expecting anyone at eleven a.m. on a Saturday morning. She had just gotten out of the shower and was heading into the kitchen to prepare some sort of brunch for herself and her son Michael.

"I'll get it," she shouted out to Michael who was just finishing up in the shower himself.

"Ok thanks mom," was his cursory reply. This morning was bringing with it many surprises not the least of which would be who was at the front door. Things were changing in the Anderson household, some would be good and some would be different. At this moment for Rachel they seemed 'all good' as her son and his friends would say, she was pleased with the turn-of-events and the surprise she received this morning at quarter past ten was a perfect example of all good.

Michael woke up at ten and looked at the clock as the first step in getting his bearings. Four hours sleep he thought to himself, four hours sleep and I'm still running on a high. His immediate surroundings threw him as he hadn't woken up in his own bed. He could hear the shower running and his eyes focused on the bathroom door in his parent's room. It was slightly ajar and he could see steam coming from around the door. The bed he was sleeping in was a mess, the sheets were no longer tucked in and the comforter was partially on the floor. The fitted sheet had been pulled away from the bottom of the bed and there was only one pillow to be found which was currently cradling his head quite comfortably. Blinking his eyes several times he breathed in deep and stretched, the room smelled of sex.

He rose from the bed and walked naked towards the bathroom. As he peered around the door he could see the figure of a person inside the shower busily going through some sort of self grooming routine. He quietly pulled the curtain back and stepped in the shower.

"Jesus!" his mother jumped as she shouted the profanity. After last night he had grown accustom to hearing her say much more colourful words of expression. "Michael I damn near cut myself."

"What are you doing?" he asked with a sly smile.

"I'm shaving. What do you think I'm doing?" She continued to move through her routine as though he wasn't there. Her back was to him as she allowed the water to rinse the remnants of the foam away from her now smooth skin.

"Well since you're in here you can hand me the shampoo," she told him, her voice full of playful tones as she chastised her son in mock admonishment. "And you can wash my hair while you're at it."

Michael handed her the shampoo and she quickly flipped the lid. She took his hand and poured what she felt was an appropriate amount of the shampoo in his palm. "Ok, now get to work my pretty." She was mocking the witch from the Wizard of Oz; she hadn't done that since he was little.

"I thought the witch wasn't supposed to get wet or she'd melt away," Michael said as he began to gently rub the liquid into her hair at the scalp. He allowed the foam and suds to form and spread the lather down her head and into her hair, massaging her head and neck as he went.

"The only things being washed away right now are my inhibitions," his mother informed him.

Rachel for her part was feeling more and more aroused as Michael massaged the shampoo into her hair. She had gotten up earlier than Michael as she was a little more use to late nights and early mornings. She decided that while he was sleeping she would take a shower and freshen up. Her underlying hope was the previous day's activities would continue, in which case she'd like to feel nice and fresh. As always she started by shaving her legs and arm pits and then became a little more brazen and shaved her entire pubic region bald. A few wild and kinky ideas raced through her head as she removed all the hair making her sex completely bald and smooth from front to back. It was as she was touching up her vaginal area that Michael came into the shower frightening her half out of her wits. Now that he was washing her hair from behind, she decided to use this opportunity to play. She began to seductively rub herself against him, grinding her buttock into his sex. The effect was almost instantaneous, his erection became quite pronounce as it was pressed between the two glorious half moons of her perfect ass.

"Mom, I don't think I can concentrate on the task at hand if you keep this up."

Rachel placed both her palms against the shower wall and used the leverage it gave her to grind her ass harder into Michael. Her hips moved back and forth and up and down his length in a sensual seductive figure eight that brought the tip of his penis from the mouth of her sex up and over her sexy little rosebud and through her firm round ass cheeks. Back and forth she continued this dance using the water from the shower and the suds from the shampoo as a sexually enticing as the opening salvo in her conquest of his raging hard on.

"Do you like the feel of my ass sliding along your cock baby?" her voice was a soft squeaky tease and it drove him crazy. His shaft continued to slide between the two halves of her perfect round ass. The bulbous head of his cock grazing over the dark rose bud of her anus caused electric shocks of pleasure to course through both their bodies.

"God mom you're driving me crazy. I can't be responsible for my actions if you keep this up."

"Why baby, whatever do you mean?" Her tone was playful and mischievous. She pushed hard into him trapping his now fully erect cock between her beautifully round buttocks.

"Oh fuck mom."

"You like that baby?" He pushed back harder into sliding his shaft back and forth through the crack of her ass. She knew she was pushing things too far and he wouldn't be able to control himself.

"I told you I won't be able to stop myself if you keep this up."

"What baby? Is mommy doing something nasty?" Her dirty talk always aroused him and drove him crazy. In a few moments she would have him exploding all over her round glistening ass.

"I'm going to do something nasty in a moment." His tone was deliberate and almost menacing if not foreboding.

"What would that be baby? What nasty thing would you do?" Her tone on the other hand sounded innocent and naïve, something she was far from being. She loved playing with him teasing him, it was something she enjoyed and missed dearly in her life, her other life before Michael.

"This!" and with that he thrust forward mercilessly hard, driving his cock deep into her ass a little more than half its terrible length.

"Oh fuck! You bastard!" The shock and pain she felt did two things to her almost simultaneously. First her body's protective reaction was to move forward and away from the painful onslaught. Second and this was the somewhat disturbing part, a rush of adrenaline surged through her giving her a heighten sense of arousal, causing her nipples to instantly harden, her sex to flood and her arms to fly forward placing her palms against the shower wall bracing herself so that she could push back.

"That's it mom take my cock." Michael met his mother's shove fully, feeling the head of his cock falter and stall.

"Oh fuck. You fucking big dick bastard." She groaned as his cock pressed further into her ass. "God you're stretching me! My ass is on fire."

"Fuck mom you're so damn tight." His eyes rolled back as he couldn't believe the sensation he was feeling. He really enjoyed fucking her vaginally but this was good too. Different, not so much better but he would definitely be doing this again.

"Easy baby you really are big. Let me get use to you." Her ass was full of cock and as much as it hurt it strangely felt good too. She knew she would have to be careful he was much bigger than his father and definitely bigger than anything she had stuffed up her ass before.

"Fuck mom. Fuck!" his impatience was getting the best of him and he was finding it hard to be the considerate lover. He held his cock still allowing her to get use to his size but the burning desire to thrust was extremely compelling.

"Ok, ok slowly now. Just go slow and I'll tell you when to speed up." He was listening now which was good but she knew he'd take control soon. She only had a short time to set the pace and then he'd want to fuck.

Slowly his cock went deeper and the strokes began to be more deliberate and steady. He was definitely enjoying this. "Awww Fuck you're going to take it right up to my balls now." His tone was sounding more and more dominant.

"That's it baby more." She said encouraging him knowing his pace would increase soon and she would be into the fucking of her life. God where did he get the stamina? His strokes were more deliberate, smoother and quite controlled he was definitely becoming a masterful lover.

"Aw that's it, that's it take my cock." The warm water from the shower continued to pour over them making his mother's ass slick and shiny as he buried his cock deeply with her.

"More baby more," she pleaded as the sensation through her body became more and more pleasurable. Anal sex had never really been her thing but she had conceded in the past and allowed Michael's father to fuck this before but again like everything else with Michael the experience was again different, more pleasurable, and more intense.

"Faster fuck me faster!" His cock moved much more quickly now deep full strokes penetrating her so deeply. She had never felt this full of cock and she liked it. She was quickly becoming aware that she was becoming his and that both exhilarated and terrified her.

"Finger my clit. Fuck you bastard finger my clit!" She grabbed his hand from her hip and brought it forward to her sex. She pressed his finger into her and pushed hard grinding her clit. The erotic buzz from this act thrilled her; she was more aroused than she had ever been wanton, wild, and sexual.

"That's it baby make mommy your bitch fuck my ass!!" The words coming from her mouth seemed all at once alien. Who was this harlot, this desperate bitch who was whorishly fucking this young man? She met each thrust fully taking his cock deeply inside of her. She was his to do with as he pleased and she found that thought strangely arousing even if it did degrade her.

"I'm going to cum mom." He immediately held still after that announcement. But she wouldn't have it she pushed back hard and continued to fuck herself on his large appendage. "Oh you fucking bitch your ass is so fucking tight."

"It's ok baby, cum if you need to, mommy can take it." Again she continued to push back and grind her ass against him taking him deeply inside her, stretching her anal passage as she had her vaginal canal. He was her lover and her bod belong to him.

"Cum baby, cum for mommy." That was all it took, with those words he was done. She had learned a long time ago that she could control the duration and pace of sex by merely saying the right choice words at the right time.

"Oh fuck. Oh fuck." He moaned and froze as his cock ejaculated deeply inside his mother ass. He knew he could never stay away from her he would be her lover and she his for the rest of their lives.

"Oh god baby I can feel you spurting in me. That's it cum for me make me yours. Make me yours." She pushed back hard driving his cock deep into her bowels. His pubic bone was pushed hard against her tail bone. His balls tightly pressed against her pussy. Her legs began to shake and she began to cum as well, a first for her she had never had an orgasm from anal sex before.

The house was air-conditioned which allowed her to wrap herself up snugly in the oversized housecoat.

"Hi can I help you?" Rachel said as she looked at the beautiful young blonde girl standing before her. Right away Rachel found herself fighting the reflexive jealousy that coursed through her body. This girls wasn't much taller than Rachel, had an all over tan that was magnificently accentuated by the outfit she wore. Whoever she was she knew how to dress in a way that subtly put all of her best attributes forward, especially if she was trying to impress a boy. The white T-shirt she wore had blue striping on both shoulders with a matching blue stripe that went down the front. It traveled over her right breast drawing attention to its shape and firmness. The T-shirt had the shorter girl sleeves and a hoody that bunched up slightly as it draped down her back highlighting her blonde hair even more. Her faded hip hugger jeans

"Is Michael home?"

"Yes he's just getting out of the shower," Rachel responded flatly. Her first response was to say she had the wrong house and slam the door shut

"Can I tell him whose calling?"

"Jessica"

So this is the girl.

The End

Share your thoughts with us.
Take a moment to tell us how we're doing. Your feedback really matters.

You can reach us by:
Email: <u>*my777books@yahoo.com*</u>

Search for other titles by **Sophie MacDonald.**